The
Thunderbolt
Pony

Other books by Stacy Gregg:

The Princess and the Foal
The Island of Lost Horses
The Girl Who Rode the Wind
The Diamond Horse

The Pony Club Secrets series:

Mystic and the Midnight Ride
Blaze and the Dark Rider
Destiny and the Wild Horses
Stardust and the Daredevil Ponies
Comet and the Champion's Cup
Storm and the Silver Bridle
Fortune and the Golden Trophy
Victory and the All-Stars Academy
Flame and the Rebel Riders
Angel and the Flying Stallions
Liberty and the Dream Ride
Nightstorm and the Grand Slam
Issie and the Christmas Pony

Pony Club Rivals series:

The Auditions
Showjumpers
Riding Star
The Prize

www.stacygregg.co.uk

The
Thunderbolt
Pony

Stacy Gregg

HarperCollins *Children's Books*

First published in Great Britain by
HarperCollins *Children's Books* in 2017
HarperCollins *Children's Books* is a division of HarperCollins*Publishers* Ltd,
HarperCollins Publishers
1 London Bridge Street
London SE1 9GF

The HarperCollins website address is:
www.harpercollins.co.uk
1

ISBN 978–0–00–825701–9

Typeset in Baskerville MT 13/17 pt by
Palimpsest Book Production Limited, Falkirk, Stirlingshire
Printed and bound in England by CPI Group (UK) Ltd, Croydon CR0 4YY

MIX
Paper from
responsible sources
FSC
www.fsc.org
FSC® C007454

This book is produced from independently certified FSC paper
to ensure responsible forest management.

For more information visit: www.harpercollins.co.uk/green

My heartfelt thanks to clinical psychologist Hilary Mack for his support and advice, and to Suzanne Winterflood, who kept my feet on the ground in this year of earthquakes.

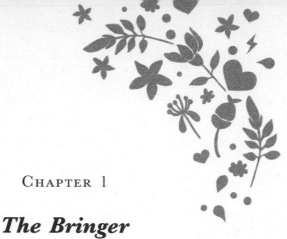

CHAPTER 1

The Bringer

On the top of Mount Parnassus, in the grand temple where the gods hang out, I am struggling to load my thunderbolts into the two white sacks strapped on to Gus's back.

"Stand still!" I use a firm tone with my pony as he fidgets. "This is hard enough without you messing about." The thunderbolts have these sharp, pointy edges that make them almost impossible to stuff into the sack and I'm trying not to jab Gus in the flank, but I'm in a desperate hurry. The white fluffy clouds beneath my feet are trembling. The whole mountain is shaking from the bottom up. There isn't much time – we need to get out of here.

"Evie!"

A voice booms through the temple and I turn round to see Zeus striding towards me across the clouds, white robes flowing behind him.

"Put the thunderbolts down, Evie."

I ignore him and continue packing. I can't stop now and leave the job half done. That would drive me mad. Two thunderbolts absolutely must go in each sack. Two plus two. An even number. I must get the ritual right, do it in sequence, or terrible things will happen. But then terrible things are already happening. The ground thunder is coming. I can feel its rumble beneath my feet, unstoppable and uncontrollable.

"Evie –" Zeus is beside me – "I want you to tell me how much anxiety you would feel, on a scale of one to ten, if you stopped doing this right now?"

His voice is soft, reassuring, and suddenly I realise that beneath his big white fluffy beard Zeus is not a Greek god at all but actually Willard Fox, my psychologist.

"Evie," Willard says, "this is the OCD trying to trick you. I know you want to make everyone safe, but you cannot control what is to come. There are things in the universe beyond your powers…"

I feel tears prick my eyes when he says this. I want to stop the rituals. I don't want to be OCD's slave any more, but I'm so scared. And the earthquake is here now. The shaking that has been rocking the mountain is growing stronger and the air around us turns electric as the thunder rolls under our feet.

Laden with his pannier bags full of thunderbolts, Gus has been getting more and more agitated and suddenly, with a panic-stricken jerk, he wrenches free of my grasp. I lunge at his reins.

"Gus!"

He gallops off and I break into a run, chasing after him, but then the clouds disintegrate beneath my feet and suddenly I am wheeling through the sky. It's like falling from a plane. Air rushes by me with incredible speed. I look down and I can see Parnassus far below. Not Parnassus the Greek mountain, but my own Parnassus. The small South Island town in New Zealand where I have lived for all twelve years of my life. Parnassus looks very different from above. I can see the rust-red rooftop of the town hall, and the dairy, and Wrightsons farm supplies, and along from the shops is my school, five classrooms set out in a horseshoe, and the chestnut trees bordering the green expanse of the playing fields. The main street looms up towards me as I plummet headlong. Even as I'm falling, in my death plunge I get this sense of wonder, because there's something cool about seeing the town from above. It all looks so tiny, but then Parnassus is pretty weeny. Mum says the tourists blink and miss it when they drive through on the way to watch the whales in Kaikoura, further up the main state highway where the road hugs the coastline of the Southern Ocean.

I can see our farm as I free-fall. The big oak marking out the lawn beside our villa with its green roof and the driveway to the stable block and the steel grey of the milking sheds. It must be almost milking time because the cows are coming in, moving slowly down the track to the shed as Jock, my Border collie, runs behind them. He's barking his head off and the noise of his bark is almost as loud as the rumble of the earth, and even though I am in mid-air I can still feel everything shaking.

The green fields are coming towards me super-fast now and I brace myself. I take a deep breath and prepare for the fact that I'm about to crash-land head first into the ground...

And then, with a jolt and a heave, I wake up.

I'm surrounded by pitch black. Something heavy is crushing my ribs and pinning me down, and beneath me the ground is bucking and rumbling with a noise like a train.

It feels so raw and so close this time in the darkness, lying here on the ground in a pup tent, with nothing between me and the rolling, turbulent earth. It was different in the first quake two days ago. I was asleep that time too and the quake threw me clean out of bed. I remember grabbing my backpack and me and Jock running for our lives as the house collapsed and feeling the cold jolt of realisation that Mum wasn't with us, then turning back and seeing her lying on the lawn, not moving. That was the quake that destroyed Parnassus and started all of this. The evacuation and my mum being taken away in the rescue helicopter, the others taking the inland road to meet the rescue ship at Kaikoura.

They all wanted me to go with them, but I couldn't. I had to make my own way. I chant the names in my head: Parnassus, Hawkswood, Ferniehurst, Hundalee, the Stag and Spey, Kaikoura. This is our journey. Me and Gus and Moxy and Jock...

"Jock?"

The heavy weight that's been squashing my ribs gives a whimper and I realise it's him on top of me.

As he struggles to stand up, he shoves his paws deep into the soft bit of my stomach. I give a squeal as his claws dig into my flesh, but before I can push him off me the ground gives another hard buck that throws both of us flat. The impact leaves me winded and I can't get any breath into my lungs. I begin to hyperventilate and it's like I'm going to die from not breathing and the more I think about dying the more I can't breathe and I begin to make these choking, gasping cries.

You want to know where I am right now on a scale of one to ten, Willard? I am a million!

And then the ground stops. I lie there, panting like a dog and shaking. My heart is hammering in my chest and I still can't get any air into my lungs. I'm gulping, trying to make my breath work again. And then my hot skin goes goosebumpy as I feel something cold and hard against my thigh. Torch! I grab for it and as soon as I have it in my hand I flick the switch and suddenly the tiny black space of my pup tent is illuminated. The first thing I see is Jock's eyes shining back at me in the light and I nearly scream at the sight of him because he looks deranged, all wild and wolfish with his hackles raised. He gives this low, panic-stricken growl, and at the same time another sound choruses in, an awful howling noise like a baby bawling. It's Moxy. She must still be in here somewhere, but even with the torchlight on I can't find her.

"Moxy!" I begin to burrow through the bunched-up folds of sleeping bag.

"Moxy?"

Moxy has worked herself head first into the bottom of my sleeping bag. I worry that she's dug herself in so deep she's going to suffocate, but when I try to pick her up she hisses and lashes out with a paw, swiping viciously at me. I take her seriously since I still have scars on my arm from the last time. I leave her alone and unzip the tent and squirm out of the flap with Jock behind me and then zip Moxy in. I don't want her to escape and get lost.

Outside the tent the night is totally black. There's not a flicker of light, no houses for miles in any direction. Parnassus is not exactly bright-city-lights, but the hills of Hawkswood are really remote. This is the middle of nowhere and it's just me and my cat and my dog. And somewhere, out there in the dense black nothing that surrounds us now, is my horse.

When the big earthquake, the seven-point-eight, shook me out of bed in Parnassus, there was a full moon to see by. Tonight the moon is clouded, the stars seem faint and distant, and the beam of my torch is gutless, so I can't see more than a couple of metres in any direction. For all I know, the earthquake might have destroyed the land all around me. Maybe everything has slid away and right now I'm perched on a cliff edge. I shine the torch beam as far as it can go and stand rooted to the spot. I turn slowly round, trying to find the tree that I tethered Gus to before I went to bed.

"Gus?"

No answer. I keep circling with my torch beam and then I see the tree. The torch beam wobbles as I search for him.

"Gus!"

My heart sinks. There's the branch where I tied his rope off, and the rope too, but I can't see him.

My eyes blur with hot tears. I'm having trouble breathing again.

The rope is frayed at the end where he strained and broke free. I feel bad when I think about how terrified he must have been to destroy the rope. But of course he was afraid. I had Jock and Moxy with me when the quake struck. Gus had no one.

This is the second time that Gus has been alone when the quakes rolled. The first time was the big one, back in Parnassus. Was it really only two days ago? It feels like a lifetime ago now. When Mum was about to be airlifted to hospital in the helicopter, she told me that Gus would be fine on his own. But she never saw how he was after the first quake struck, the pure terror in him. He'll be feeling that same fear again right now, and once again I've let him down because I wasn't with him.

I should have slept with him. Like a Bedouin nomad who brings his horse into his tent to sleep right beside him for safety. That's what I should have done with Gus.

He's an Arab – you'd know that straight away if you saw him, with that delicate dapple-grey coat and skinny ballerina legs and his pretty dished face. I should have taken him inside my tent, except it's only a pup tent and it's way too small. It could barely fit me and the dog and cat. So why didn't I sleep outside under the tree with him? We should never have been apart. This is all my fault. Who leaves their best friend alone like that?

I shine the torch around again, like I still expect Gus to magically appear beneath the tree. Then I walk back to the tent with Jock hugging so close to me he's almost wrapped round my thigh. Working dogs usually stick close, but Jock is like glue and I know he's worried that we're going to lose each other too.

"Good boy," I reassure him with a pat on his

head, and then I bend down and unzip the tent very carefully, making the smallest gap possible to let us both back in and at the same time make sure Moxy won't bolt out. We've been through enough in the past few days and I don't want to lose her again. I want to look for Gus, but first there's something I need to do. I can see Willard Fox at this moment looking down from the clouds still dressed as Zeus with his beard and everything, frowning as he tells me that OCD is a war. "In a war, Evie, you can't win every battle. Sometimes you have to accept a loss or two. But you can still win the war."

On a night like this, my OCD is too hard to fight. And so I give in to the urges, and once Jock and I are back inside the tent and all zipped up, I begin the rituals.

I pick up my backpack and undo the side pocket. Then I do up the zip and then I unzip it again. Unzip-zip-unzip and already I feel a lot better. My heart isn't pounding so hard in my chest any more, but my hands are still shaking as I take the contents out of the pocket and lay them in front of me in the torchlight. There are four items: a gold pen that writes with blue ink, an old takeaway container, a pair of glasses and a pocket notebook.

Somewhere out there in the dark, Gus is lost and I need to find him. But I can't go yet. I want desperately to go and search for my pony, but the rituals override logic and compel me to continue.

I line up the objects like precious artefacts in a museum. I check them and rearrange their position and then I stack them back in the pocket of my bag in precisely the right formation and I zip it up again. I do this twice over, and then I am done. My heartbeat slows further. I can breathe now. The air goes in and out and there's a lightness in my chest. I am ready.

When I emerge from the tent this time, I have my backpack on and I feel better because I've done things right. All the same, I feel like it still might not be enough protection. And I know I should have done more last night before I went to bed.

If I'd done the rituals better then maybe this earthquake wouldn't have come.

If Willard Fox was here right now, he'd tell me

that my rituals are not going to change the world... that they wouldn't stop an earthquake. I am not responsible for saving the fate of others or even myself. "Evie," he'd say, "do you really think a twelve-year-old girl can unleash catastrophe? That you are capable of killing everyone you love and care about, including Jock and Moxy and Gus? Because if you can do this, Evie, then I'm pretty sure that one of those super-secret spy agencies like the CIA would have got in touch with you by now. They could use someone like you. Powers of mass destruction. They'd want to harness that, right?"

The way he says it, it isn't cruel or sarcastic. He's not mocking my abilities. Willard is truly asking me the question. Do I really in my heart believe it's because of me? Am I the one responsible for all of this?

Sometimes I believe him and I know it's not real. Other times, like right now, I lose faith, I fall back on the rituals.

I know I could have done them better. But it's been hard because I'm not at home any more. I'm in a tent, camping out, with no one around to help me and everything keeps changing. I am trying to do it right but I know I've been failing.

The gods of Parnassus up high on those fluffy clouds are watching me and they see it. They know it's all my fault. That is the burden of my powers, and if Willard was to ask me right now at this very moment if I caused all of this I would tell him the truth and say, *Yes, yes of course it's me. It's always been me.*

My name is Evie Violet Van Zwanenberg and I am the harbinger of a power so dark that, if I cannot control it, I will destroy the world. I am no ordinary twelve-year-old girl. I have thunderbolts in my fingertips and lightning in my veins. I am the end of days. I am the bringer of earthquakes.

CHAPTER 2

One Year Ago – How I First Became a Thunder God

I walk the blue line with Mum beside me in the hospital. It traces our path on the linoleum floor past A&E where feverish, pale children sit quietly beside their anxious mothers. Past the x-ray rooms where they plaster the bones broken in trampoline accidents. Then through the double doors and we are on the main ward, and as I walk I cast my gaze through an open curtain and I see a girl about my age lying asleep in her bed with tubes in her arm and in her nose, and I think, "Poor kid, she looks sick."

That's the thing. I don't think of myself as being like her. But I'm in hospital, aren't I? There is something wrong with me. You just can't see it.

15

We keep walking through another set of double doors, still following that blue line, and now we are in a reception area and the sign on the wall by the desk is printed in clear black type on white: Adolescent Mental Health.

Mum approaches the nurse. "I have Evie Van Zwanenberg here for her ten am appointment with Willard Fox."

I don't like it here. "Hospital" is supposed to be where you go to get made better, but to me it's a place where people go to die.

I'm in the same building now where my dad used to be. Only to get to his ward we used to follow a different line, a red one. It would take us through from the car park and the heavy double doors along the lower corridors to the lifts.

I remember the first time I came with Mum to see him after they'd moved him on to the ward. Mum led me through the corridors along that red line until we reached the lifts and we stepped inside this massive metal chamber and she pressed the button for Level 8, and I looked at the word on the sign on the wall and sounded it out in my head and I asked her, "What's oncology?"

I know what it means now. Oncology is another word for cancer. That's what they found in my dad's spine when he went to see the doctor about the back pain he kept getting when he was milking the cows.

Even when I knew the word, I didn't really know what it meant. Looking back now, I feel unbelievably stupid because I had actually found it fun making those family trips from Parnassus to Christchurch each week. Mum and I would drop Dad at the hospital and then we'd go for lunch in Container City – which is the part of town where they have made all the shops out of these big shipping containers. They did it as a temporary thing because all the buildings were destroyed in the earthquake seven years ago, but then it remained and I kind of like it the way it is now. There's a really good noodle bar in Container City so usually we'd have noodles and mostly we'd get takeaway noodles for Dad too for later.

Things changed once he was on the ward and he didn't get to go home. We'd still get him noodles but he never, ever wanted to eat them. He wasn't hungry because of the medication he was on. Mum kept buying them anyway, even though he'd just leave them sitting there going cold beside his bed. By then the cancer had metastasised. That was another word I didn't know. It meant it had spread, travelling from his spine to his liver and his brain.

Me-tas-ta-sised – that word sucked all the air out of the room when they told Mum. She couldn't look at me as we walked back to the car without Dad that day.

I remember how, when she unlocked the car, she kind of crumpled over for a minute and didn't get in. I had this lump in my throat that wouldn't go away, and when I opened my door and sat down in my seat for some reason it seemed like the right thing to do to shut my door not once but twice. Then I did the same to my seat belt, buckling and unbuckling, doing it up twice too – click-undo-click.

Looking back, I can't tell you why, but from that moment on the way home from the hospital when I double-shut that car door, that was when it began. I did the same thing when I got out of the car at home. I shut the door and then opened it and shut it again. I thought Mum would ask me what I was doing, but she didn't even notice. I guess she had other things on her mind. Anyway, from then on it wasn't that I wanted to do it. *I had to do it.*

Mum didn't notice at home either when I shut my bedroom door twice. In the morning she told me off because I'd left my bedroom light on all night and I said I'd fallen asleep but really it was because when I went to switch off the light, I had this urge for making things even, just like the car door, and I found it impossible to only press the switch once so I had to switch the lights back on again, and off and on again to make it even, and then the lights were still on and so I slept with the lights glowing and my head buried in Moxy's fur.

Every time from then on, when I got in the car or entered my bedroom, I completed that double door slam and on the second swing as the lock clicked shut I felt this incredible release. It was like a rush to my brain, this surge of energy that felt solid and real, and in that perfect moment I knew that somehow my actions were making everyone that I loved – Dad and Mum and Gus and Jock and Moxy – safe.

Double-slam, double-slam. I didn't realise that pretty soon the urge for release would become my prison. That when I tried to stop doing things twice it would throw me into an anxiety attack that made me feel like a swarm of bees was invading my brain, the buzzing inside my head making me want to scream and curl up in a ball and disappear forever.

As the rituals took hold of me over the coming months, I desperately wanted to tell Mum what was happening to me. I mean, I was so scared of my own mind, I really thought I was going crazy. But what if I *was* crazy? And what if Mum found out I was having all these weird thoughts and she stopped loving me? You know, they have mental hospitals where they lock up kids like me – I've seen it in movies.

The more I thought about telling Mum, the more afraid I got. And the more I double-slammed those doors.

I couldn't tell Moana either, even though we were best friends at school. I told Moana once about how I'd wet the bed on school camp and she told Juanita Wanakore and she teased me about it all term. If I was going to tell someone, I had to know I could trust them to never tell another soul.

I remember when I told Gus, he just held me with his eyes. I sat on the five-bar gate and I stroked his neck as I spoke and I told him everything. I knew he was really listening because the whole time his ears swivelled back and forth and his dark, liquid brown eyes were soft and sad and sometimes he wrinkled his muzzle. And as we sat there together, I very carefully did two tiny braids into his mane at the base of his neck by the wither. And that was when I knew that Gus was a part of my OCD too, and that I needed to do these two braids to make sure that Gus was safe. They would protect him, and even Jock and Moxy too.

When I first got Gus, he came from a farm where he was in a big herd of horses. I thought maybe he'd miss having a herd, but when he came to live in Parnassus, it was like me and Jock and Moxy became his herd. With Gus and Jock, they have this real respectful relationship. Like, when we go for rides across the farm, Jock will always fall in at Gus's heels and keep in time with his strides. Border collies are smart like that and Jock is super well-trained. He used to be a working dog until he got too old, and I can give him instructions and he does whatever I tell him.

Moxy is the wild one of the group – she always runs ahead, being our trailblazer, sniffing and scouting the way. She's intrepid for a cat. It's in her breeding. Cornish Rex are real explorers. If you don't know what they look like, well, they are almost bald because they have this crinkled-up fur like they've been shaved and the skin stretches taut so you can see the bones of her skull through it and she's super-skinny with a long, ropey tail like a rat. I'm not making her sound very beautiful and I guess she's not, but she is kind of amazing-looking, like the sort of pet an Egyptian princess would own.

We paid almost a thousand dollars for Moxy, and Dad was furious when he found out because he said he could buy a good working dog for that and you can get kittens for free around here because people are always giving them away. You shouldn't have to pay for them. But Mum said Cornish Rex weren't like ordinary cats – they were explorers, more like dogs than cats in their way, and loyal like a dog is loyal, choosing just one master. Also she knew this lady in Christchurch who was a "cat fancier" who bred them and did us a cheap deal. She was a really odd woman – she kept her cats in cages and washed them in special shampoo and wouldn't let you play with them and when you went round to her house it smelt of cat poo and all her furniture was covered in plastic.

Dad soon changed his mind about paying for a fancy cat once Moxy chalked up the highest kill rate of any ratter we've ever had. She's an amazing huntress. And she eats the rats too. Lots of cats will eat mice but not rats because rats taste gross, I guess, but Moxy swallows them down – she crunches up everything except for the fangs at the front and the tail at the back.

Moxy is supposed to be my cat, but if she's loyal to anyone it's Gus. She thinks she belongs to him. Or maybe it's the other way round and she thinks Gus is her horse. If I'm looking for her then I'll find her out there in the paddock with him, curled up on top of his rump, purring contentedly.

Gus was the only one I told about my OCD for a long time. In fact, I never would have told Mum at all. I was going to keep it a secret forever. The problem was, the OCD got worse. It got so bad I began to lie about stuff. Like, I would pretend to be sick and just stay in bed all day because I figured if I didn't move, if I did nothing at all, then I didn't need to do any of my rituals and I wouldn't have to try to fight the urges inside me.

Only Mum wouldn't leave me alone. She kept insisting that if I wasn't actually sick, I needed to go to school and do my chores. But the OCD made it impossible because I'd developed this complex world of chaos in my bedroom. It looked like a big mess, but it was all part of my plan and I'd lie in the middle of the floor like a statue with the lights as bright as heaven above, unable to switch them off and trying not to think as the bees made my head fuzzy.

One morning Mum came into my room. I'd had the lights on all night and when she left my door open and touched the light switch I started shouting. It all suddenly burst out of me like pus from a swollen wound.

"Mum!" I began sobbing. "There's something wrong with me!"

It was Mum who looked up my symptoms on the internet and discovered I was OCD. The initials stand for Obsessive Compulsive Disorder.

"Evie," she said, "it's going to be OK. We'll find someone who can help."

That was what led us back to the hospital, following the blue line this time instead of the red. Once a week every Tuesday at four.

We come here, to these familiar corridors with their weird, tainted smell that is a mix of antiseptic and blood, and every time I catch sight of that sign in the lift that says "Level 8: Oncology" I feel the tears well up and I get so mad at myself, and I tell myself not to cry. I tell myself all sorts of things. And I count my footsteps. One-two. Even steps between each floor tile, an even number of buttons that must be pressed when I enter the lift, and two whole glasses of water from the cooler in the waiting room before I enter Willard Fox's rooms to begin our session.

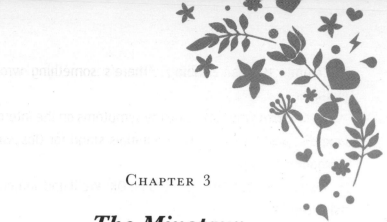

Chapter 3

The Minotaur

I still can't believe Gus is gone. I stand beneath the bough of the tree where I tied him last night before I went to bed and then I walk round the tree again until I have done a full circle, as if this is some insane game of hide-and-seek.

I shove my torch under my armpit to free up my hands so I can untie the remaining length of rope that he left behind. When I touch the frayed ends where the rope has been broken off, it makes me feel sick. Poor Gus! He must have been terrified to rip it apart like that. It would have taken such force! He must have pulled back like mad when the quake struck. Terrified and alone, desperate to escape.

I work the rope free, prising it off with my shaky fingers, and all the while Jock stays with me and squashes so hard against my thigh I can feel his heart pounding through his bony ribcage. I lower my hand to his head and stroke his ears to soothe him with my own trembling fingers. He gazes up at me and gives this desperate whimper and we look each other in the eye and I know what he's thinking because I'm thinking it too.

"It's OK," I say. "We're in this together and we will find him."

Anyway there's no way we can make it to Kaikoura where the rescue boat will be waiting without him. And it won't wait forever. Time is already running out. So we have to find him, and soon.

But I don't even know where to start, here in the dark in this paddock somewhere between Hawkswood and Ferniehurst, the remotest hill country of the South Island coast. No people for miles, no houses, no lights.

I desperately want to go back into the tent and

curl up in a ball and cling on to Moxy and stay in the tent with her and Jock. Then we could look for Gus when the dawn comes. But I can't do that. I think of my pony out there on his own and I know he's scared and he's in trouble and I can't abandon him to survive the night alone. Darkness or not, I'm going to find him.

One thing on my side is that Gus is a smart horse. Back at home in Parnassus, when I fetch him from the paddock, I don't need to go far because I can call him to me. So even out here in the middle of nowhere, I know that if he can hear me, he'll come to me.

And so I call him.

"Gus!" My voice breaks in the night air and it sounds so frail I hardly recognise it.

"Gus!" I try to be stronger this time. I need the sound to travel as far as it can for him to hear me.

I don't keep shouting. I pause for a minute and wait to see if he will whinny back to me. That's what he does back home. Gus is clever. He's always known his name. He knew it even before me, from the very beginning…

"So you didn't name him Gus?" Willard Fox asks me.

"No," I say. "He was already called that when I got him. You never change a pony's name. It's bad luck."

"And you're superstitious about it, huh?"

I raise an eyebrow, as this seems like a dumb question. I am superstitious about everything.

"What sort of riding do you do with Gus?" Willard asks.

"He's really good at cross-country," I say. We've jumped one-star fences at home, which is really big for a 14.2 pony. I think he's good enough to make Eventing Champs.

"His actual competition name isn't Gus. It's Pegasus. I just call him Gus for short."

"Pegasus!" Willard Fox exclaims. "Nice. Like the horse in the Greek myth?"

"Well, Pegasus was white and Gus is kind of, well, he's dapple-grey," I say. "And so they're the same except the Greek Pegasus had wings and he was born from the neck of the Medusa to be the carrier of thunderbolts for Zeus."

Willard Fox looks impressed. "So you know your Greek gods?"

28

"We're studying them at school."

I thought Willard Fox would be different from this. A psychologist should have a white coat or a stethoscope or something. Willard Fox wears a plaid shirt and jeans and his hair sticks up all scruffy and he's got this smile that takes up his whole face. He gives me one of his big grins when he says, "You must be really upset to be missing school," but I don't smile back.

"I'd rather be in school," I say.

"Really?" He doesn't look at all offended, he just shrugs it off. "OK, cool. So this whole psychologist thing is all your mum's idea, huh?"

I don't reply.

"So why don't you want to be here, Evie?"

"Because," I say, "I don't even have OCD."

Willard nods. "Fair enough," he says. "Tell me, why are you so certain, Evie, that you don't have OCD?"

I frown as I think about this. "Well, I don't ever care if my hands are dirty."

Willard nods thoughtfully. "So that means you can't have OCD, right? Because people with OCD are clean freaks, right? They wash their hands all the time and they keep things totally neat. And they say things like, "Oh, I simply have to keep the kitchen spotless because I'm sooooo OCD!"

He waves his hands about theatrically as he says this and I can't help laughing.

He sees me laugh and he smiles too and his goofy little-kid grin takes up his whole face again.

"Evie," Willard Fox says, "it's not about being a neat freak. There are lots of different ways to be OCD. So tell me about you. Let's talk about what you do."

Then there is this enormous vacuum in the room where I say nothing for ages and Willard Fox just sits there and he says nothing too. And he waits and waits and when I speak at last my voice is all trembly.

"I count things..."

***

I shine my torch into the darkness in every direction but I can't see Gus and I am just thinking I should give up when Jock, who is still glued to my side, lets out this low growl.

"What is it?" I say.

Jock growls again, and this time it's in the back

of his throat, and the growl gets lower and lower until it becomes a bark.

Grr-woof, grr-woof!

I put my hand down to touch him and realise that the hackles have risen up on the back of his neck. Does he sense that Gus is near or is it something else? "What's up, Jock?" I ask him.

The only time I've seen Jock act like this is when an aftershock is coming. And so I brace myself for the boom and the rumble beneath my feet, but then when it doesn't come and he's still growl-barking I know there is something out there. It must be Gus.

Jock tenses up. He wants to go, but I'm worried I'll lose him too! I grab his collar to hang on to him and he strains against my hand as I take the rope that I pulled down from the tree and I tie it on to him.

A Border collie knows one hundred and sixty words. I remember Dad telling me that. I've always wondered how many words Jock really knows. I know he knows my name, and his. I'm pretty certain too that he knows "Gus".

"Jock," I hold his muzzle in my hands as I speak to him. "Go. Find. Gus."

When I let go of him this time, I feel the rope go taut in my hand and he pulls me forward with a lurch. I stumble to keep up and I train my torch beam on to Jock's back so I can follow him. I'm surrounded by darkness except for his blurry black and white form that moves ahead of me through the void.

The rye grass is long and damp from evening dew and I feel wetness seeping through above the top of my riding boots as I half walk, half jog to keep up with him.

I can feel the anxiety creeping up on me, making my pulse race. I hope the braids in Gus's mane have held. I can't do anything about them now, but there are other rituals I can do. I could stop again and arrange the contents of my backpack to squash the anxiety back down. But I push through the fear and keep going, even though my mind is racing with thoughts like *What if we get lost? Then we'll never find our way back and Moxy will end up trapped in the tent alone and she'll be stuck in there forever and she'll starve and die...*

…and just as I'm running all the worst-case scenarios through my head and I'm about to lose it, Jock stops running. He freezes in front of me and the hackles on his neck stiffen straight up and he starts barking his head off. But when I shine the torchlight ahead of us, there's nothing there!

What is he going on about?

"Gus?" I call out.

"Gus!"

I shift my torch to the left and there in the clean, white beam of light he stands facing us. His white face is dappled like the moon, dark eyes reflecting and unblinking.

If I had hackles like Jock, they would rise on the back of my neck too. Because the eyes captured in my torchlight are not the ones I expected. The fur is grey like Gus, but the face is broader and coarse, and gleaming above his temples there are two sleek, hard horns, lethal and as highly polished as sabres, curving and sharpening to a brutal point on either side.

Jock growls and the creature returns my dog's warning with a threat of his own – a deep, indignant snort expelling streams of mucus from his nostrils.

This is not my horse. Not Pegasus at all, but the Minotaur. I am staring at the face of a great, white bull.

CHAPTER 4

The Sacrifices

The white bull stares back at me, his eyes boring down my torch beam. For a moment, we hold each other's gaze. And then I run!

Almost immediately I know it's the very worst thing I could possibly have done. Idiot! I curse myself for turning my back on him. But the fear is so deep and so primal, I'm not thinking, I'm just falling and getting up again and scrambling for my life, running through the deep grass and then tumbling forward, down on my hands and knees, panting and sobbing, as I try to escape.

I can hear Jock behind me and he's barking his head off! He didn't run after me. The herding dog blood is so strong in him, he's instinctively turned to face the bull. I've seen him do it before. Once he dominated a whole stampeding dairy herd and turned them round by holding his ground. But a white Charolais is not the same as a Friesian cow, and even a working dog with Jock's awesome skills can't back him off for long. I hear my dog's valiant woofs and in reply come the angered snorts of the bull. There's silence, a stand-off of sorts, and then the ground shakes and I think *aftershock*. But it's not an earthquake this time. It's the lumbering gait of the bull.

I turn with my torch and see Jock, unbowed and unafraid, facing him down and barking like mad.

The bull stops for a moment, and I think maybe Jock has him. But then he lets out this bellow, and the noise is so strong and low and terrifying, it's like a lion's roar. And then there's the thunder of hooves once more and with my wobbly torch trained on the bull I don't entirely see, but I know that he's got Jock!

I can hear him yelping!

"Jock!"

He keeps howling and I know he's been hurt and

without thinking I find myself running back to him. My heart is pounding, and all I care about now is Jock and reaching him before the bull can get him again.

I run through the dark, stumbling and falling and getting up again until at last I reach Jock's side. I stand over him and spin round in a full circle looking for the bull, making myself dizzy following the torch beam, hyperventilating with fear. Where is he? Where did he go?

Then my torch casts a shadow and I catch a flicker of something white in the furthest reaches of the beam. It's the bull! He's about ten metres to the right of us, and he's moving in our direction.

At my feet Jock gives a whimper as if he's trying to say, "You run!"

I can't run, though. Not without him. So I throw my torch to the ground and yank my sweatshirt over my head and for a second everything is black and I'm panting and blind, and then with a tug my sight returns and I snatch up the torch in my left hand, and with the sweatshirt in my right, I focus back on the bull.

The sweatshirt is blue, which I know is the wrong colour. It should be red, right? Like a matador's cape. But I am hoping that waving it around will have the same effect.

"Hoi!" I call out to the Charolais. "Hey, Bully Bull!"

I hold my sweatshirt out as far away as I can from my body and I wiggle it.

The bull pulls up to a halt, he stamps a hoof. He's looking at me.

"No!" I say. "Not me. See the sweatshirt? Look at the pretty sweatshirt!"

The bull prepares to charge. As he angles his massive forehead towards the ground, the horns rise up and I see their gleaming, bony tips and I realise far too late how ridiculous I am with my matador cape. The bull is ten times my size and the sweatshirt is like a postage stamp to him.

I fling the sweatshirt hopelessly in his direction and I throw myself to the ground on top of Jock. And as the hooves thunder I know that any moment I will feel the impact. I've seen bulls attack cattle dogs. I once saw one on the farm get gored by a horn and he had to be put down. And that's what I'm thinking this bull will do to me, and I can feel Jock squashed beneath me and I think at least he will be safe because the bull will get me first.

And at that moment I am Theseus, facing the Minotaur.

***

I'm back in the hospital for my second session with Willard Fox. I'm telling him about the Ancient Greek day we had at school.

"I went as the goddess Athena," I say.

We had to dress as gods so I wore an old bed sheet knotted at the shoulder, and when I got on the bus George the bus driver gave me a look and said, "Your mum forget to wash your clothes?"

Half the kids on the bus weren't even in costume.

"Moana was just in shorts and a T-shirt!" I tell Willard Fox. I was grumpy with her that day because we had a fight about superpowers.

"I said my superpower would be to jump those really

huge four-star cross-country courses like at the Badminton Horse Trials," I tell Willard Fox. "But Moana said horse riding's not a superpower, even though it totally is."

"So that's why you had a fight?"

I shake my head. "No, we had the fight after that."

Moana said her superpower would be mind reading and to show me she put her hands on my head with her fingers splayed at my temples. And that was when I panicked and pulled her hands off me because if Moana could read my mind then we wouldn't be best friends any more. She would think I was a freak because of my OCD.

"So Moana doesn't know you have OCD?" Willard Fox asks.

"No," I say.

No one at school knows. Especially not Mrs Lowry, and sometimes it's hard because she picks on me because I can't write certain letters – like M and N. And so my spelling is bad.

At the Ancient Greek day, Mrs Lowry got Brodie to do the sacrifice to Zeus – because he's her pet and he gets to do everything. But I am doing sacrifices too, every day and no one cares.

The counting and the rituals... even my bedroom. Mum

thinks it's a "god-awful mess" but really it's my gift to the gods, a complex matrix of talismans and portents disguised as dirty clothes and old bowls of half-eaten cereal. And, then there's my backpack, the most precious piece of my OCD universe. And those two braids in Gus's mane. I must do them. I have to get them just right. If I don't manage to ace it all – then I unleash hell.

"Evie, what if I told you that this is all the OCD? And it is tricking your brain. What if I told you that even though it seems real, your rituals don't have the power to protect people?"

Willard Fox leans forward. "You're doing this because you really love your animals, don't you, Evie?"

I nod. "Of course I do! More than anything."

"Well, what would you do if Gus got really sick?"

I feel my pulse quicken. I don't like to imagine bad things happening to Gus.

"I'm protecting him," I say abruptly. "He's not sick."

"Yes, but accidents happen, right?" Willard says. "So let's say Gus gets hurt in the paddock. He cuts his leg. How would you fix it, Evie? Would you use your powers and do the braids in his mane? Pack things in and out of your backpack? Or..."

Willard Fox looks at me. "Or... would you maybe call the vet?"

I feel my cheeks turn hot. When he puts it that way I know that it is illogical, what I am doing.

"I'd call the vet."

Willard looks at the backpack that I have beside me at my feet.

The force of my panic surprises me.

"Don't touch it!"

"It's OK..." Willard Fox says. "I know it's precious. How about you show me?"

My hands are shaking as I pick up the backpack and put it on the table.

It sits there between me and Willard, like an unexploded bomb.

"Now what?" he says.

"I have to do the zips," I say. "I do them twice. Before I take the things out."

"OK," Willard says. "So that's the OCD talking. And today, we're not going to give in to it. Today, instead of doing it twice, Evie, I want you to just unzip the zip and close it again once and then leave it. Can you do that?"

I reach out my hand, slowly, and when my fingers touch

the zipper the bitter rush of pure adrenalin makes me want to be sick. Just the once? That's so dangerous!

I close my eyes and I take a deep breath and I do it! I unzip the front pocket. Just once. It's sitting there gaping open – taunting me! Then I zip it shut again. Just the once! It's so wrong. I can feel the bees surging in my brain, imploring me to do it again, to make things even!"

"You're doing great, Evie," Willard Fox says.

Ohmygod ohmygod ohmygod!! I hold my hand there, wanting to unzip-zip it a second time, tantalisingly close to giving in to the urge to do it again. It takes every bit of my willpower to fight it and all the time I can hear Willard's voice talking me down, but it sounds fuzzy through the buzz of the bees in my brain.

"On a scale of one to ten," he is saying, "where are you now Evie?"

"...eight," I pant out the word. "I can't breathe!"

I want to make the world safe!

"Evie," Willard Fox says my name like he's invoking a god. "You. Can. Do. This! I want you to say out loud with me: 'I'm in charge, OCD. I'm taking the reins!'"

I look at him and I feel a lump in my throat that blocks the words.

"Come on, Evie!" Willard says. "You don't want to be controlled like this so do something about it. You need to fight it. Do it!"

And there, in the middle of his office, I hear his voice and then I hear another voice and it's mine but it doesn't sound like me. I'm screaming. "I'm in charge, OCD. I'm taking the reins!"

When I finish shouting the words, I burst into tears. Great big gasping sobs, and Willard is right there with me, telling me it will be OK and to take breaths, big deep breaths.

"Good work, Evie," he says to me. "I'll see you next week."

***

Fear is not static – it is a living thing. Like the earth beneath my feet, constantly moving and changing. It sounds crazy, but looking back, at that moment in Willard's rooms the zip on my backpack was just as terrifying to me as this half-a-tonne of Charolais bull in front of me is.

In the beam of my torch, the bull is bearing down

on me. I know what's coming and I'm about to close my eyes and brace myself for the death blow, the sharp stab of the lethal point of the horn into my gut. But the impact doesn't come.

Thunder rolls through the ground once more and I look up and see a pale shadow appear from the darkness, galloping its way towards us and coming between me and Jock and the bull. In my torch beam, the grey dapples bleach away so that the horse looks almost white and the tail that unfurls behind him is flecked with stars. He looks like a creature from a Greek myth himself, like Pegasus. But he's totally real, and my heart soars.

It's my pony. It is Gus.

CHAPTER 5

Pegasus and Athena

G us charges in at a gallop, and he pulls to a halt right between me and the Charolais. I see his eyes, dark and burning, as he squares off against the bull, and I feel the hairs on the back of my neck stand up at the heat of the desert blood in him. Gus taunts the Charolais, flashing back and forth in front of him in a high-stepping trot, then circling around, keeping just far enough away so that the bull cannot reach him. I keep my torch trained on them and its beam becomes the spotlight illuminating a grand performance as Gus dances rings around the Charolais. The dance is deadly, but there's such grace and beauty to it. He spins and arches his neck,

46

hocks driving beneath him so that one moment he almost seems to trot on the spot and the next he's flying forward, his mane whipping in the vortex created by his acceleration. I have never seen him look more Arabian than he does at this moment.

Compared to the fluid beauty of my horse's movement, the Charolais looks like an old, punch-drunk prizefighter who's been beaten too many times in the ring. He's a lumbering oaf, slow and witless. He staggers around, bewildered by Gus's display, and then, shaking his enormous head as if he's been dazed and suddenly woken up, he gives a snort and charges. He is too slow. Gus is already gone, and the bull misses completely and now Gus loops behind him and circles round and round, still just out of reach in his high-striding trot, and then as he dashes past once more he shoots off, moving purposefully away from me and Jock so that the bull gives chase. They disappear into the darkness and that's when I know we have our chance to get to safety. I grab Jock by the collar and we run.

Jock is on his feet and he's matching my stride. I

still don't know how badly he's injured from the bull's strike but despite his wounds he can move well enough. He bounds on in front of me, leading the way, and my torch beam is wobbling so that the world seems to fling about in front of my eyes but I keep running. Then up ahead of us I can see the tree where I tied Gus last night and I know we have somehow found our way back to camp.

My fingers fumble to unzip the tent. I can hear Moxy yowling her distress inside. I scoop her up in my arms, and she does this thing she does when she is really, really pleased to see me where she bites my face. And then she even smooches all over Jock, which is unusual because she's mostly a bit stand-offish with him and not all cuddly like she is with Gus. I see her sniff at Jock's side, examining him, and he whimpers and begins licking the spot with his tongue and I can see now where the bull got him. There's a cut on his flank where he got nicked by the tip of the horn. Even though there's blood, the wound is shallow. If I was a vet I don't think I'd even do stitches, and Jock is licking it clean so he will be OK.

Jock and I lie there beside each other, both of us panting, exhausted from running all the way back, Moxy purring all around us. I shine the torch on my watch and see that it's four am. I want to get out and search for Gus again but it would be better to wait until it's light. At least I know he's close now and we can find him when the dawn comes, but I'm not going back into the dark with the bull still out there. Gus can outrun him, I'm certain of that. But we're not as quick. And so we lie there and when I get my breath back, I pick up my backpack and I zip and unzip it again. I do my rituals, until my heart is beating at the regular pace once more.

Not all rituals are bad. Mum used to say it was "our ritual", whenever we went to see Willard Fox, to stop off on the way back in Parnassus at the dairy to get an ice cream.

If my friend Gemma was working, I'd always get a single cone of vanilla because Gemma does big scoops. But if Scary Mary was behind the counter then I'd have to go for a Choc Bomb because Scary Mary's scoops are too stingy.

Scary Mary owns the Parnassus Dairy. She doesn't let you browse the *Horse & Pony* either. She has a grumpy handwritten sign up over the magazine section that says: "Please purchase *before* you read. This is not a Library."

Anyway, I'm in my tent doing my ritual with the backpack, and I'm thinking about Willard Fox and the very last time I saw him. We were rating all the things that give me OCD on a scale of one to ten, and then Willard Fox came to my backpack.

"On a scale of one to ten," Willard Fox asks me, "where would you put the backpack, Evie?"

The backpack is my portable OCD world. You could take the sum of all my fears and shove them together and they would fit neatly inside that backpack. I look at Willard Fox. "A ten."

"Evie," Willard says, "I feel like we've been here together in the foothills for a long time now and you've done all this stuff in preparation, and now you're ready. It's time to go up Mount Everest."

I know what he wants and it makes the bees in my brain start humming.

I mutter something about how I've done enough. My

OCD is much better now, and maybe I don't even need to come and see him any more, but Willard Fox still wants to look inside my backpack.

"What's in there?" he asks me.

"It's personal," I say.

Willard Fox leans forward, his elbows on his knees. "Do you know what rust is, Evie?"

"Like on a car?" I say.

Willard Fox nods. "The thing about rust is, if you remove it, you have to get rid of all of it because if there's still a little bit of it left then it grows back again."

He looks at me. "OCD is like rust. We need to get it all out..."

"Or the OCD will come back again..." I finish his sentence.

I clutch the backpack to me. "If I let you look inside," I say, "it will ruin it."

Willard Fox nods. "Do you want to tell me then?"

I take a deep breath. "There's a pen," I say, "and a takeaway container, and a pair of glasses and a notebook."

"And why these four things?" Willard Fox asks.

"Because I like even numbers."

"Why else, Evie?"

There's a pause in the room and you can hear the clock.

I listen to it ticking. Willard Fox is good at silence, though, and he holds on and he waits for me.

"They were on my dad's beside table," I say. "In the hospital. When I did it."

"When you did what, Evie?" Willard Fox says.

I don't answer.

"Evie, do you think you made something bad happen?"

I am shaking. I look down at my hands and see that they're bound in a tight knot. This was why I never wanted to come here! I knew it would come to this eventually. Willard Fox is too smart for me. I knew he would find out what I've done.

"Yes... no... maybe."

"Well, that covers all the bases," Willard Fox says.

I haven't admitted this before, not to Mum or even to Gus. But with Willard the words just come out before I realise I've said them.

"That day when we visited Dad," I say, "I... I was trying to stop having the OCD and I... I made myself do it."

"What did you do? What do you mean, Evie?"

"I didn't know it would happen! I was trying to be good."

There is no air in the room and the dust motes float

and I am not in my body any more. And I can hear my voice but it sounds like it isn't mine as I tell Willard Fox what I did.

"I came home and I got out of the car and only slammed it *once*. And that was when it happened."

I'm in tears now, and I can barely sob the words out.

"That was the day he died."

"Evie? Do you really think your dad died because you didn't slam a car door twice?"

He's not being funny right now and his smile, for once, is gone.

"Yes," I say softly.

Willard Fox leans forward and makes a steeple with his fingertips. "You know, if this was Ancient Greece, we could have blamed the gods for your dad, right? Maybe your sacrifice to Zeus wasn't quite right. Or maybe you angered one of the other gods, like Hera, maybe?"

I nod, my eyes misting with tears.

"Things were a lot easier, I think," Willard Fox says, "when we had gods to shoulder the responsibility for our fates. Because without gods, how do we explain famine and disease and war? Or the death of someone we love.

53

Without gods, there is no reason. All we have is the randomness of life. So why does fate make our car tyre go flat, or make our horse go lame just before a big competition, or give us the cancer that kills us?

Willard Fox hands me a tissue and I blow my nose.

"Evie, your OCD wants you to believe that you can slam a car door twice and change the course of the future, that you are the mastermind of this universe, that your rituals will bring order. But they won't. So here's the deal. You have to accept that the world is beyond your control. Stop making sacrifices to fake gods and take back your real power."

He smiles at me. "Can you do it?"

I sniffle a little and then I look him square in the eye and I say it: "I'm in charge, OCD. I'm taking the reins."

And this time, I really, really mean it.

***

"Are you ready, Evie?"

It's the weekend after my last session with Willard Fox and I'm in the best place in the whole world. At the start line of a cross-country course.

Mum is standing beside me with Gus in his full tack.

He has a martingale on him, and his new cross-country tendon boots. I pull on my gloves and tighten the chinstrap on my helmet, and then Mum gives me a leg up. I feel a rush run through me as I land lightly in the saddle and slip my feet into the irons.

My OCD has been bad this morning. As I was tacking up, I could hear the bees ready to swarm and at the last minute I caved in to them and hastily put two tiny braids into Gus's mane after all. No big deal. Just to be safe. To be safe. Now, as they're calling out my number, 23, I get another twinge of OCD. I look down at my bib and wish it was an even number. Even would be safer. Even would be good.

"Two riders to go ahead of you..." Mum looks at number 21 who's at the start box and about to be given the signal to set off on the course. "You can head down there now..."

She smiles and gives Gus a slappy pat on his shoulder. "Remember to slow down into the woods to take the roll top," she says. "You need to give his eyes a chance to adjust to the light in there. Evie, remember at the ditch, look up! Never, ever look down or he'll stop. Your eyes will take you where you want to go..."

At the warm-up area beside the start box I take a tight

hold on Gus and look out over the fences and trace my battle plan in my mind. Mum and I have already walked the course twice this morning. There are sixteen jumps and it seemed to me that her advice for each fence was usually exactly the same. "Sit up, keep straight and kick on!"

I ride laps of the warm-up arena, first at a walk to loosen Gus's limbs, then at a trot and finally at a canter. I pop him over the practice fence five times until Mum gives me the thumbs-up and we are both confident that he's ready and feeling keen as he pulls against my hands.

I'm ready too. My brain, always buzzing, always in turmoil, has suddenly become as clear and bright as a summer day and all I can see is the cross-country course laid out in a perfect map in my mind. I can feel the power of the horse beneath me at this moment.

The starter beckons me into the box. I put the reins into my right hand and place my left hand over my wrist to set off the watch.

"On your marks, get set..."

Gus anticipates the "Go" and he surges forward. In two strides he's into a fast canter and we're careening down the grassy hill and then I'm checking him back and kicking him on again as we come back up the dip. Ahead of us in four strides stands the rustic. I want to count the strides into it, but as Gus sees the fence his ears prick forward with enthusiasm and his canter begins to roll out, brave and bold, and he gives a snort and shakes his head to reef the reins free as if to say, *Leave it to me, I've got this.* And so I do. I keep straight and I kick on after that, but I don't try to second-guess Gus any more or tell him about striding, because he knows better than me and we are a team, him and I, and you have to trust your pony.

We have a wobbly moment at fence number four, which is a sunken road where you drop into a ditch and then put in two strides and jump out the other side. Gus is quite short-striding so he ends up sticking in three and I get left behind a bit and he bangs his leg on the bank as we exit, but he's fine. I don't even lose my stirrups and I'm back in two-point position and I check my watch and we're still good on time.

At the downhill combination Gus has found his groove as he flies the massive fantail and then bounds down the bank and up and over the ditch and the log, and we're back on track for the final four fences and on the road to home. I can feel his breath coming hard now. The course is almost two and a half kilometres and he's getting tired. When I check him before the next fence, he gives a tempestuous snort, as if he knows he's near the finish and he wants to keep running despite the tiredness in his limbs. We take the big oxer, and the picnic table. One fence to go. My stopwatch is beeping. I am right on the timer – it will be close.

The last fence is next to the warm-up area, and as we swoop in towards it I can hear my name being called over the loudspeaker and I feel Gus suddenly perk up as if he's no longer tired at all and as we come in to take the roll top he picks up and stands off before the fence and flies it! Despite the early take-off, I'm with him this time, and as we gallop on and sweep between the finish flags, I hear my watch give a final beep. We have made it under time.

It's only after we've cooled down and I've led Gus back to the float that I realise his two braids have unravelled. They're completely gone. They must have come undone on the course. And the realisation that me and Gus, we did it all on our own makes me so proud. But it worries me too, because I have no idea how long our protection was gone. Hastily, I put the braids back in again, just hoping that I'm not too late.

***

That night, I Blu-Tack the rosette that we won on the wall of my bedroom. And then I lie on my bed and I look at it, and I ride that cross-country course over and over again in my head. I feel every twist and turn on the course, every undulation and hill, and most of all I recall the fences, the way Gus boldly attacked them on a forward stride with me rising up in my stirrups and giving him his head, that delicious moment of suspension in mid-air above the fence when we were no longer earthbound at all. We were Pegasus and Athena. The winged horse and the goddess. Immortal and brilliant, in a world of our own...

I'm so tired and my muscles are so sore that when Mum shouts out and asks if I am ready for bed I lie to her and say yes, even though I'm still in my jodhpurs and boots because I'm so exhausted and so happy staring at my rosette. I fall asleep like that, fully clothed. As it turns out, this is lucky.

Moxy wakes me up making this strange mewling sound and I can feel her trying to burrow hard into the blankets.

I look over at the bedside clock. Fourteen minutes past midnight.

And then the room begins to tremble and there's this dark rumbling beneath me, a roar like a train is coming. I'm thrown out of bed and I hit the floor with such force it's like someone has punched me in the guts. I gasp for breath and I try to stand but the floor under my feet is undulating now. It's like trying to stand on the waves of the sea and I fall back to my knees. That's when the adrenalin brings me to my senses and I know I'm not on a train and this is not a dream. The world is falling apart around me and I am going to die...

***

I wake up with a gasp as if I've been submerged underwater and am panicking for breath. This is how I always wake up now, since that night in my bedroom when the first earthquake happened. It takes me a moment to realise where I am, and then I feel the hardness of the ground beneath my tent, and the damp seeping through the nylon of my sleeping bag and I remember. We're in a paddock somewhere between Hawkswood and Ferniehurst on the road to Kaikoura and last night there was another aftershock and Gus got loose and there was a bull…

Through the thin nylon walls of the tent, I can see that it's light outside. How long have I been sleeping? I need to get up and search for Gus. I reach out a hand and feel Jock lying beside me. He has his head at this end of the tent, right beside mine, and Moxy is curled up on the other side of my shoulder so that if you looked down on us from above right now we would look like one creature all joined together. We are Cerberus, the three-headed dog.

The three-headed dog gets up. Moxy is dying to get out, and as soon as I unzip the tent she bolts across the grass. For a moment I'm blinded by the brightness of the sunrise and I rub my eyes, and when I open them again I can see Gus. He's grazing on the grass right in front of the tree where I had him tied last night. Moxy has already reached him and she is smooching up against his muzzle.

When he sees me, he gives a nicker, like really casual, as if he'd been there all along!

I go over and sit down in the grass beside him, with Jock and Moxy – the four of us, together again – and we stay like this for a bit, but I know we have to go. I'm just about to rouse myself and pack up the tent when Gus suddenly raises his head and Moxy crouches low like she's afraid and Jock begins to whine. And then, a few seconds later, the ground rumbles beneath us.

It's not a big one, this aftershock, it doesn't last for more than a couple of seconds, but it's enough to get me straight up on my feet. It's a reminder of what we've been through and where we are now and why we need to keep moving. And as I put the two braids in Gus's mane I chant the names: Parnassus, Hawkswood, Ferniehurst, Hundalee, the Stag and Spey. Kaikoura lies ahead of all of them. We have a long way to go.

Chapter 6

Seven-Point-Eight

There's no sign of the bull as I pack the tent ready to leave. Moxy waits until I'm done strapping the tent and bags on to Gus, and then she vaults through mid-air to take up her position behind my bedroll on his rump. I lead Gus back through the paddock, making sure to shut the five-bar gate behind us, and we are on the wide grass verge that runs alongside State Highway One, heading once more in the direction of Kaikoura, with a sign ahead of us that says "Ferniehurst".

Round the bend in the road the earthquake has left wide cracks in the tarmac, as if Zeus has been sending his thunderbolts down to earth and they've split the road in jagged seams.

Gus shies and spooks at the cracks. I have to urge him on, and he has his ears back, and as he vaults over one of them I try to peer down it, wondering how deep the fissure goes. Will I be able to see all the way to Hades? But then I get anxious because Moxy has jumped down off Gus's rump to examine the crack too and I think she might try to clamber in and then I'd never get her out again. There's no one else on the road except us. The roadblocks on the damaged Parnassus bridge have diverted all the traffic inland on the Leader Road. Mayor Garry took everyone that way. He said that no cars could get through on State Highway One. But I'm not in a car, am I? On horseback these cracked and broken roads can still be travelled.

The aftershocks seem to be growing more frequent and I'm not sure what that means. I feel them happening almost every hour right now. I'm becoming strangely attuned to their rhythm. I know when one is about to strike because Jock will give the early warning. I'll hear him let out this weird, low growl

64

and his hackles will rise. And then a few seconds later, it comes in the distance. This sonic "boom" like a bomb going off and then the aftershock follows the sound and the ground begins to shake. They are little earthquakes. Not like the big one. The one that threw me out of bed that night back in Parnassus.

***

I hit the floor so hard I'm winded and I can't breathe. I try to stand again, but I'm thrown back and this time I slam both my elbows as I hit the carpet and cry out in pain. I hear a loud yowl in my ear and feel the scratch of Moxy's claws as she scrambles and vaults over me on the ground. I can only just make out her shadowy shape as she sprints out of my doorway into the blackness beyond. There's no light in the house, the power must have gone out.

On my hands and knees I crawl in the same direction as Moxy. Over the top of the piles of clothes and the plates. Something large and solid in front of me blocks my path. It's my backpack. Without even thinking about what I'm doing, I sling it over my shoulders and continue on towards the doorway.

My hands grasp the door frame and I think about staying there. At school they tell you doorways are safe places, but when the floor beneath you undulates like waves you don't feel safe and your brain tells you to run.

I can't get my balance to stand up so I crawl down the hall, panting, scurrying on my hands and knees. I feel bare floorboards and then something sharp crunching against my shins. I wipe my hands across my jodhpurs and feel a vicious stab in the palm of my hand. Broken glass on the floor! A vase has fallen and shattered across the hallway. If I wasn't still wearing my jodhpurs there'd be cuts all over my knees from the shards. I stand up and wobble my way down the rest of the hallway, hands bouncing off the walls as I reel from side to side.

"Evie!"

I can hear my mum's voice above the roar. That train-engine noise is actually coming from under the house! Echoing and booming through the rooms, filling the darkness with thunder.

"Evie! Where are you?"

"Mum? Mum!" I can see her on the far side of the kitchen, near the front door. She sees me too. She tries to come back for me and I watch her lurch sickeningly and fall against the walls and pick herself up again just as I've been doing all the way down the hallway from the bedroom.

"Evie!" she screams at me. "Come on!"

Mum is not a big woman. She's not much taller than me. But when she grabs me in the kitchen as the floorboards shake us, it's like I'm being swept up by a grizzly bear. She flings her arms round me and almost yanks me off my feet and I feel the power in her grasp lifting me off the rollercoaster as she drags me towards the front door.

We're both outside on the veranda of the villa and I'm stumbling down the stairs and then suddenly at the bottom step I realise Mum isn't there any more. She's back on the veranda with Jock. He's tied up there and she's furiously working to undo the knot of rope on the buckle of his collar but it's impossible because he's straining against it.

"Jock, down!" Mum commands and, despite his fear, Jock obeys. He's a working dog and even in a state of panic he follows orders.

I begin to run back towards the steps to help her. Mum sees me coming and she shouts at me. "Evie, no! Get clear of the house and stay away from the power lines. Do it! Now!"

I look up and see the row of tall power poles that run down the driveway to our house swaying like saplings in a high wind. I turn and run towards Gus's paddock. I'm almost at the point where the driveway forks and leads to his gate when suddenly there is Jock! He's at my heels and he's running hard, and I know that Mum must have got him free. We're panting and heaving together and the ground is still throwing us about like we're toy ships on a real ocean.

Jock is with me, running. And then I realise. Where is Mum?

"Mum?"

Then from behind me there comes a new sound, louder than the train roar that woke me, louder than the rumble of the earth that continues to rock beneath my feet. This is the sound of an exploding bomb.

I stop running and turn round.

"Mum..."

I'm thinking Mum must still be in the house. Except... except there is no house.

It should be there. The tall peak of the corrugated iron

roofline, bordered by the square outline of the veranda, should be casting a shadow in the sky, but it's gone. And that's when I realise that the sonic boom that I heard a moment ago was the sound of the house collapsing in on itself. In its place, there's a hole where my house used to be. Our villa has been brought to the ground, the ruins jagged and black against the night sky.

"Mum!"

I'm running hard now, back from where I just came, towards the wreckage of what was once my house. The last time I saw my mum she was standing on the veranda!

"Mum!" My screams, louder than the train-roar, turn to a hoarse whisper.

"Mummy?"

There. By the front path, there's a dark shape on the ground. It's not moving. It's her.

I run to her, throw myself to the ground beside her and shake her.

"Mum!"

She groans, lifts her head. "Evie?"

I feel a rush of relief. She's alive!

"Mum..." I am crying. "What happened?"

"I..." Mum pushes herself up on her hands. In the back

of my mind, I am aware that the ground is no longer rumbling. Everything has gone quiet. I can hear my breath coming hard and fast, my blood pounding.

"Something hit me," Mum says, "in my back."

She's breathing hard. "Evie, I think my leg is broken. I can't move it..."

As she tries to push herself up on her forearms, I see her face turn white and she whimpers with pain.

"Mum!" I say. "Don't try to move. You have to stay still."

A moment ago, in the rush of fear that she was dead, I shook her awake, but now I am remembering my first aid from pony club. If she's broken her back, any movement might paralyse her.

"Don't move, OK?" I say. She doesn't reply.

"Mum?"

She's blacked out. But I can see her breathing and I know that she's alive.

"Mum?" I try to rouse her again, not by shaking her this time, just gently rocking her shoulder. She murmurs.

"Mum, stay here and wait for me. Don't move. I'm going for help."

There's a full moon tonight. A burning orange globe in the sky that illuminates the farm just enough so that I can see where I'm going as I run back up the driveway. My heart is slamming in my chest. The adrenalin surge that struck me when I was thrown out of bed refuses to release its grip. It makes my brain move at double-speed so that everything around me seems to go into slow motion. When I enter the tack room and reach for Gus's bridle. I can see my hand pick up the bridle and I disconnect, as if someone else is occupying my body and it's not actually my hand at all. I look at my saddle and think there isn't time. I leave it and don't bother with the helmet either. I cross the driveway and climb the wire-and-batten fence and drop to my knees on the other side and then get up and wipe myself off and scan the field for Gus.

I can hear him before I see him. His hooves are pounding out a frantic drum beat in the night air. He comes towards me, head held high, tail even higher, nostrils flared and ears flattened in terror as he tries to find solace in the one thing a horse must do if danger is near. He is running.

"Gus!"

When I call his name he doesn't hear, he's too overwhelmed. I stand in the paddock and block his path as he gallops towards me and for a moment in the darkness I wonder if the moonlight will be enough for him to see me. He's gone wild, so deranged by fear that even if he sees me, he may still trample me.

"Gus!" I hold firm as he keeps bearing down on me, but my heart is slamming against my ribcage. Does he see me?

I wave my hands above my head, making myself as big as I can, and I see his strides falter and slow, and then with a jerk he slams on his brakes and goes back on his hocks and pulls up.

He's trembling all over, his eyes wild, nostrils flared wide. Sweat foams on his neck and his flanks are heaving. How long has he been running like this?

"Gus," I murmur. "It's OK, it was an earthquake but it's over now. It's over now and I'm here..."

I hear my own words coming out of my mouth and it's like I'm acknowledging to myself what just happened. An earthquake. Out of nowhere, out of the blue. I have never in my life felt as much as a quiver beneath my feet before, and now I'm standing in my pony's paddock and my house – just a few metres away, where I was asleep in bed less than ten minutes ago – is in ruins and my mother is unconscious on the ground and the power lines still threaten to fall.

And how do you explain to a horse what has just happened? My Gus, my poor Gus, is beside himself. I can see the whites of his eyes and he's making this whinny that I've never heard a horse make before. It's the sound of pure fear.

When I reach to touch him, he jerks back like I have electricity in my fingertips. Then he lashes out violently – kicking with his hind legs.

"Gus, Gus, it's OK..." That's when my tears come. He's so terrified and I'm so helpless. But I keep trying, I keep talking to him and stroking him and slowly, like a fog is lifting from him, I see the old Gus return. His eyes change. He knows me again.

"That's right," I say, "it's me, boy, it's me, Evie."

He softens into my embrace, and I hold him, fingers entangled in the rope of his mane, face buried in him, the two of us breathing as one.

"Are you hurt?" I ask him.

He lets me run my hands over his body, as I work my way all round him, checking for injuries, but his muscles twitch at my touch, the tension in him as taut and alive as the power lines that spark and crackle beside us in the night air.

At his wither, I check his braids, and feel a wave of relief that they are still plaited tight.

I slip the reins over his neck and the familiarity of the routine, doing up the cheek strap and cavesson, seems to reassure us both. I feel my heart beat more slowly as I cluck him forward and lead him to the gate. The latch got jammed shut by the earthquake, but I keep working it with my hands until I finally feel the metal give. It comes loose and I swing the five-bar out and lead Gus alongside it so I can climb the rungs to mount up.

When I fling myself on his back, he dances a little from side to side and I hope that he's calmed down enough to handle having a rider on his back. After what we've just been through, I wouldn't blame him if he bucked me off. I keep talking to him, whispering softly that I'm here with him, telling him about Mum and what's happened and why we need to do this.

We're going to Moana's. Her farm is next to ours. Two ridges divided by a valley, with Chilly Stream in the middle. To get there on foot takes maybe twenty minutes, but I've never done it at night and that's why I need Gus. He can see better than me in the dark.

He doesn't buck but he does this stiff-legged, tense

joggy trot back up the driveway, and his spine is all bony against my bottom. Jock follows at heel, trit-trotting alongside us, and all the way I can hear the power lines overhead spitting and crackling and I worry that if they fall now I'll get tangled in them and electrocuted, but finally we get past them and we are at the gate that leads to the ridge paddock.

I lean down from Gus's back to open the gate and almost slip as he side-steps through. Jock follows too, keeping up with us. I urge Gus into a canter. It's so much easier to sit on his back at this pace as the gentle lope of his stride rocks underneath me. The moon is bright. It lights the path ahead enough for us and I trust Gus to be my eyes. I feel the wind in my face as we reach the top of the ridge and I look around me in both directions and see... nothing. I've been up here before at night, so I know I should be able to see the lights of Moana's house in one direction and the lights of Parnassus township in the other. But tonight there is nothing except the blackness. The power must be out through the whole valley.

I sit there for a moment, wondering if this is such a good idea after all. From here, the ridge makes a steep drop to Chilly Stream and it's about ten minutes to Moana's house. But I'd been expecting to have her house lights to guide me down, not to be riding out here blind.

Go back, I think. But no, that isn't an option. The house is gone and Mum can't move and I can't help her on my own.

At the top of the ridge, where the goat track descends into blackness, I lean back to keep my balance and I squeeze my legs and I cluck Gus on. He doesn't hesitate. He is so brave, he virtually flings himself off the ridge and I cling on even tighter than before because even though I can't really see much, I know that now we're on the narrow winding path that's barely wide enough for him to keep his footing down the slope. The darkness is good in a way. If I could see, it would be worse because it's a long way to fall. I don't look at all. I trust Gus to get us down, and I know when we've made it to Chilly Stream when I can hear the water gurgling in the blackness ahead of us. I hear the dogs start barking and Jock barks straight back at them and now the Mahutas' two enormous black Labradors come bounding out to see who it is. But even though they know me and Jock and Gus, they're so on edge after the earthquake that they don't let up – they're barking like crazy and their hackles are raised. The next minute I see the familiar shape of Mr Mahuta in his shorts and gumboots and tartan shirt come lumbering out of the house and then I'm blinded by a torch beam.

"Evie?"

The light is still in my eyes. The dogs are still barking and Mr Mahuta is yelling at them to shut up.

"Evie!" I know this voice straight away. It's Moana's mum. "Are you all right, sweetheart?"

The worry in her voice makes me tear up a little, because until this moment I haven't really had a chance to cry, but now I do. As she comes up and hugs me, I realise I'm shaking. Somewhere in the distance, there is a loud "boom" and then everything around us jolts and the dogs start baying again. It's the first aftershock.

***

That night seems so long ago, and there have been so many aftershocks since then. Moana and her family will be on their way to Kaikoura now too, all of them together in the car taking the inland road through Mount Lyford. And here I am, on the coast road on my own. Well, not alone. I have Gus and Jock and Moxy.

The signpost for Ferniehurst has been tilted on its side. I'm pretty sure the earthquake did that. I stop right beside it to eat lunch. I've picked up a few windfall apples from the side of the road, and I have my stale bread rolls and the cheese. Jock will take a bread roll too but I've got nothing now for Moxy since I used up the old salami. I need to find some food for her.

The road ahead gets steep from here onwards. I can see the hills rising up, blue with conifers as we enter the foothills of the Hundalees. But first we have one more river. We are about to cross Siberia.

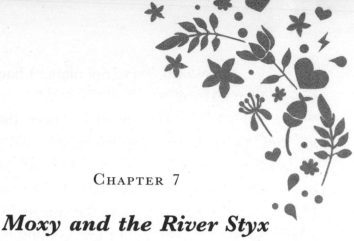

CHAPTER 7

Moxy and the River Styx

I've stopped feeling bad about having no food for
Moxy. When we stopped for lunch in Ferniehurst,
and Jock and I ate stale bread rolls, Moxy disappeared
for about ten minutes and when she returned she
had a rabbit in her jaws! She ate most of it for her
lunch then let Jock have the rest. Now she's riding
up behind me on Gus's rump once more and
surveying the roads ahead down her elegant nose
like she's an Egyptian queen being carried on a
litter. She's always loved to travel.

One time Moxy even caught the school bus. She'd
followed me up the driveway that morning as usual,
except this time she actually got on board the bus

behind me and I didn't notice her until after George the bus driver had closed the doors and driven down the road almost to the next stop. By then she was jumping on kids and running up and down and everyone thought it was hilarious, except George, who said she was making us late for school. I wanted to take her back to my gate, but George said he couldn't turn the bus round. He said, "If she's smart enough to get on the bus then she can find her way home." And he picked her up and threw her out of the bus doors, then shut them again and drove off! This was before I had my OCD. But I remember that even then I was really worried about Moxy all day at school. I was so upset because I thought she'd never find her way back home and be lost forever, but at 3:15 when George dropped me off she was there at my gate waiting for me. She's a clever cat.

Right now, Moxy is grooming herself on Gus's rump in the sun. It's going to be a hot day and I can see the bridge up ahead. Beyond that the Hundalees rise up. The hills are dark green to the left of the highway and bleached like bones on the other side. It's not far now before we begin to climb into the mountains. The road ahead is about to get tougher, and the first thing we must do is to cross Siberia.

Siberia Stream flows through the mountains all the way from St Arnaud down to the coastal plains of Conway Flat. Most of the year, Siberia isn't much more than a stream, but in the months when the snowcaps melt it becomes a wide, fierce torrent, choppy and deep.

The bridge over it looks fine from a distance, but as I ride closer I see what the earthquake has done, how the metal barriers on either side have buckled and twisted, and how the tarmac surface of the bridge has giant cracks in it. In places you can see all the way through to the stony riverbed. There is no way you could drive a car over it. But I'm on a horse and so I cluck Gus onwards. He doesn't want to move at first, but I coax him until he steps out, first with one hoof, and then another.

They chime out a hollow sound and Gus spooks and side-steps, and as he does this, I feel the bridge shake beneath us.

We're only a little way across at this point, but I can already feel the whole structure shaking! I look ahead of me at the massive cracks in the tarmac, and I swear they're getting wider as we stand here. And then Jock, who's still at our heels, starts up barking. I mean, he's going crazy, really barking his head off, and instead of staying back behind Gus, he suddenly rushes ahead of us, which is something he never does. He goes out in front of Gus and he stands there right in the middle of the bridge. He's still barking at us, like a heading dog trying to turn the cattle round.

"Jock, stop…" I begin to tell him off, but then I hear the creak of the concrete pillars beneath us and I feel the bridge lurch to one side.

My heart is racing but I try to go slowly as I rein Gus backwards. I don't want to turn him or move too quick as any movement in either direction could make the bridge beneath us collapse.

"Steady," I say as I back him up step by step. "Good boy."

Once we're off the bridge, I dismount and Jock comes running to me. I hold him close and I can feel his heart pounding against my leg.

"Good boy," I whisper. "Good, Jock. It's OK."

Only it's not OK, because if we can't use the bridge then how do we cross? The stream is swollen with icy water right now and the river rocks are treacherously slippery underfoot. But what choice do we have? We need to get to the other side and there's no way I'm going over that bridge.

I lead Gus down the steep bank of gorse and scrub that takes us to the riverbed. I look straight up at the underside of the bridge and see the tangle of steel spaghetti that's been ripped out and exposed like guts spilling from beneath the concrete, and I realise it's a miracle that it didn't collapse when we stood on it. One good aftershock is all it will take for the whole thing to fall.

Down here the river rushes in a furious surge and the bridge above acts like an echo chamber compounding the roar of the water. Gus doesn't like it, and as I mount he snorts anxiously, skipping about.

I urge him away from the cover of the bridge, further upstream, and then steer him down to the water's edge. The stream is at its narrowest here and boulders stick up above the white froth. I'm not sure how deep it is. Surely it isn't too deep for Gus to walk through it?

"Come on," I coax him. Gus dances a little. He's a good cross-country horse and never afraid of a water jump but this surging torrent is not what he's used to and as soon as he steps his front legs into the water I can feel him tense up in the drag of the current. He hesitates, but I kick him on because we have no choice. On his rump behind me, I can see Moxy peering down at the water. She lets out an anxious yowl.

Gus gives a snort and then ploughs into the stream. Behind us, back on shore, Jock starts whining. I turn and see him looking upset at being left behind, his ears flattened, eyes worried. I'm about to call to him when, with a bark, he leaps boldly in!

He's only just submerged when he gets picked up and swept off by the current. I watch him paddling like mad as he gets taken sideways downstream. He's fighting to stay with us and make his way across to the other side.

Gus is up to his chest in the river now and striding forward. I try to hold my legs up so that I won't get my boots and jodhpurs wet, and behind me Moxy has moved from Gus's rump to perch at the highest point on top of the bedroll, digging into the nylon with her claws for dear life.

Moxy can swim if she has to, I've seen her dive into the dam on our farm and cat-paddle her way to the other side. But this water is a washing machine, not a millpond.

We're just over halfway across when Gus stumbles into a hole. All of a sudden I feel him lose his footing and the ground drops away and it seems almost like he's rearing as all four hooves leave the riverbed and he can't touch the bottom any more.

Trying to regain his footing Gus powers forward, dropping down on his haunches and swimming, and I give up on keeping my jodhpurs dry because it's all I can do to stay with him, clinging on round his neck with both arms. We're still in the grip of the current for another stride or two and then I feel his hooves dig once more into the sandy loam of the riverbed. We're through the deep patch and back on the ground, and I'm soaking wet all the way to my armpits, but we're OK. I look back over my shoulder to check and

I see the tent and the sleeping bag still there, and then my blood runs cold.

"Moxy?"

All around me, white water churns and smashes against the rocks.

I try to turn Gus, my eyes searching the water all around us and my voice drowned out by the torrent roaring as I scream for her.

"Moxy!"

***

It's the night of the first earthquake. We're in the car going back to help Mum. I'm sitting on the bench seat of the ute, squished between Mr Mahuta and Arama, Moana's brother, and at that moment all I can think about is the fact that I'm stuck in the middle so I haven't been able to slam the car door twice and it's making me go all OCD. I can feel my heart pounding and on the radio there's this woman with a really calm voice but she's saying these really scary things about the earthquake, how it's cut Kaikoura and Parnassus off at both ends of the highway and everyone on the coast road is trapped. "We are getting reports in from GeoNet," she says, "that this was a seven-point-eight."

On a scale of one to ten, I am seven-point-eight, Willard!

I am seven-point-eight and I am worried about my mum but also Moxy is missing too. Now that I think back I never actually saw Moxy make it out of the house – what if she was still inside when it collapsed? I'm trying so hard not to cry, but why didn't stupid Mr Mahuta let me close the car door twice!

The woman on the radio is now talking about tsunamis. "Residents in the Kaikoura coast region are being evacuated to higher ground..."

My mum isn't on high ground. She's lying in front of the veranda. If the tsunami comes before we can get to her then it will be too late.

I see a wall of water rising up above her, vast and unstoppable. I feel a choking in my chest and I can't breathe. And then the tears come, hot on my cheeks. I try not to sniffle too loudly and I'm embarrassed that I'm crying.

"Evie," Mr Mahuta clutches my hand tight, "don't worry, we're too far inland. A tsunami wouldn't make it as far as Parnassus."

But it's too late to stop worrying. I'm already imagining the giant wave sweeping over her. That's the problem, because once something is in my brain then it becomes dangerous. What if I'm making it happen?

You're not the one doing this, Evie, says Willard Fox's voice in my head. *You are not a force of nature. You are a twelve-year-old girl.*

Mr Mahuta pulls up in the driveway and the car headlights strike the wreckage of what was once my home. From the way he slams on his brakes and just sits there in dumb shock, I realise he thought I was exaggerating about the house. But I wasn't. It's been flattened, destroyed by the quake. It looks like a scene from a disaster movie.

"Geez, Evie," Arama says. "How did you get out of that alive?"

Mum is right where she was when I left. "Mum?" My voice is all chokey as I run to her. My legs are shaking so much, I can hardly stand. I fall to my knees on the ground at her side.

Mr Mahuta joins me, crouching down beside her. He takes Mum's hand, feeling her pulse.

"Julia?"

Slowly, Mum raises her head. "Is that you, Harry?

Mum tries to raise herself up on her elbows and suddenly she moans.

Her face has gone really white in the headlights.

"Is it your back?" Mr Mahuta looks worried.

"No!" Mum grits her teeth. "My leg!"

She tries to push herself up on her elbows and then screams again.

"Hey, hey. Take it easy, eh, Julia?" Mr Mahuta says. "Arama's here. We'll get you up."

He gestures to Arama, "You go round that side, take her feet."

Arama looks terrified but he does what his dad says.

"OK," Mr Mahuta says, "it's gonna hurt a bit when we lift you so you just take a deep breath..."

Arama slips his hands underneath Mum's feet and before he can even pick her up she lets out this painful whimper in anticipation.

"Wait for me –" Mr Mahuta slips his hands under Mum's armpits – "on three..."

"One, two... three!"

Mum screams when they lift her up. I mean she really screams!

Arama looks so terrified, I think he's going to drop her.

"You hang on!" Mr Mahuta tells him.

They walk, stumbling across the grass, carrying Mum as she screams, and lay her down on the ute where they've put a mattress on the open-air back of the flatbed. I feel so useless as I stand there and watch them arrange her on the mattress, Mum whimpering with pain.

"Evie?" Mr Mahuta gestures for me to get on. "You climb up and ride on the back with your mum. We'll go really slow, but you bang on the window of the cab if it gets bumpy, OK?"

I climb up the tailgate to get on board. Mum has her eyes closed, but when I take her hand she opens them. "Evie?"

"Hi, Mum." I choke back the tears. I can see her leg is still sticking out at that funny angle and her hand in mine is really cold.

Mr Mahuta gets back in the cab and turns the ignition. The engine revs into life, and as it does there is another noise, so slight, so distant that it's almost imperceptible, but I hear it. And I know straight away that I'm not imagining it. I slam the palm of my hand hard – bang-bang-bang – on the window of the cab.

"No! Don't go! Wait!"

I leap off the back of the flatbed and run towards the front veranda of the house where the noise is coming from.

"Moxy! Moxy!" I call.

From underneath the collapsed boards of the veranda, I hear her strident high-pitched meow. It's like the meow she makes when she's accusing me of missing her dinnertime.

"Moxy!"

At the sound of my voice she comes running out, pelting towards me. I grab her and clutch her tightly to my chest. I'm holding her so hard I might crush her, but she doesn't seem to mind. I can't believe I nearly left her behind.

"I've got you," I say. "It's OK, I've got you. It's OK..."

And I don't let go.

***

The surface of the river churns white all around me. I can't see her anywhere!

"Moxy! Moxy!"

And then a little face bobs up just above the top of the water, about twenty metres downstream. She's right out there in the middle of the river! I can see her little paws frantically churning away, trying to stay afloat. The current sweeps her around in circles and she crashes into a half-submerged willow bough.

I watch her go under and then I see her paws reach out and grab the willow bough. She manages to climb on to it.

"Moxy!" I call to her. "I'm coming for you!"

Jock had reached the riverbank but now he throws himself back into the water too, barking at her, as if he's telling her to stay put and wait for us! *Don't try to swim. We will come to you.*

But Moxy doesn't listen, she runs the length of the bough towards the far shore and then makes an almighty leap from the branch on to a rock, and then another rock. She's further downstream now and still making her way from rock to rock towards the shore − but when she jumps from a rock on to another willow bough, the branch is too flimsy to take her. It gives way and she's in the water again! The rush of the white foam hides her for a moment as she goes under, and this time when she pops up I only make out her terrified little face for a split second before she is submerged once more.

"Moxy!" I'm up to my chest in the water and I'm struggling to the spot where I saw her last but she's gone already, swept like a leaf downstream in the swift current. I think I catch a glimpse of her, but then the water swallows her again.

And now I'm turning round mid-stream and struggling back to the bank once more.

I run alongside the bank, calling Moxy's name with Jock beside me, for what seems like hours. And then, in my cold, wet clothes, with my backpack sodden and heavy on my back I lie down in the grass and I sob. My Moxy is gone. The river has taken her, and left no trace.

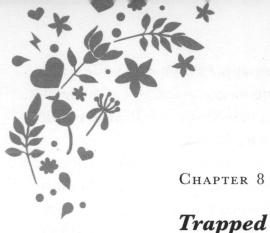

CHAPTER 8

Trapped

We turn away from the dark green hills of the Hundalees and follow the river towards Conway Flat. Jock is ahead of us, running fast, zigzagging back and forth along the riverbank, his nose to the ground the whole time. He's hoping to pick up a scent trail that will prove that Moxy washed ashore, that she's still alive.

My jods are soaked through and it's horrible riding in them, but I'm better off up here on Gus's back because I can see further this way. My eyes sweep the riverbanks in desperation. I keep having flashbacks to that moment when the tree branch collapsed, and the fear on Moxy's little face as she hit the water, tiny nose poking up above the white foam, paws churning furiously against the might of the current. She's a fighter, my cat. If anyone can survive in that river it's Moxy.

In the Greek myths, the river is a death symbol. Crossing the Styx took you to Hades. But the Styx could make you invulnerable too. Achilles was dipped in the Styx. Maybe Moxy has crossed over to Hades, but I don't believe it. She's invulnerable and we will find her.

I lost all my food in the river when we fell into that hole. The stale bread got soggy. The windfall apples were swept away. So now, after we've searched all morning and the sun rises to its midday height, we stop to rest, but there's nothing to eat. I lie down on the grass for a moment to let the sun dry my jods and then I pick up my backpack and zip-unzip-zip-unzip and do my rituals. Arrange my objects. Pack them up again. Redo the braids in Gus's mane. Yes, Willard Fox, of course I blame myself for what happened to Moxy. All I'm doing now is trying to make up for it, to protect us all and make us safe. That's all I've ever tried to do.

95

I hold Moxy tight in my arms all the way to Parnassus. We're not going back to the Mahutas' house. We're meeting up at the town hall.

The town hall is right along from Wrightsons, and Scary Mary's dairy. There's a big lawn behind the hall and that's where the gathering point is. Lots of people are there already. Mrs Mahuta sees us arrive and comes running and leans in through the driver's window to talk with Mr Mahuta.

"We've set up a medical tent. Dave is coming to look at her, he's just gone to get his medical bag from the surgery."

Mr Mahuta takes the ute straight across the lawn and parks up beside the tent, and him and Arama carry Mum, with me and Moana running alongside them. I'm still carrying Moxy because I'm scared to let her go. Jock is with me too.

Inside the tent Mrs Mahuta is preparing the camp stretcher and foam mattress with a clean white sheet on it for Mum.

"Hang tight, Julia," Mr Mahuta says as he lies her down on it. "Dave's just gone to the clinic to get his things. He'll be here in a minute."

"Dave?" Mum looks worried. "But he's a vet..."

At that moment Dave arrives back. He's a young, curly-haired man with bright round eyes. He wears his stethoscope round the neck of his navy shirt.

"Julia!" he greets her brightly. "I hear you got hit by a house?"

Mum gives him a weak smile. "I guesss I wasn't fast enough," she says.

"Yeah, those houses can move pretty quick, huh?" Dave bends down beside the stretcher bed and holds Mum's hand in his, and gives her a reassuring smile as he feels her wrist to take her pulse. "I'm going to give you something for the pain first, to take the edge off, and then we're going to take a look at the leg, OK? By the looks of the way it's sticking out, it's definitely a break, and we're going to need to move it back into position and put a splint on it to make you more comfortable."

Mum, pale as a sheet, exhausted, looks around the tent at all of our faces as if she's expecting us to intervene, but no one says anything as Dave pulls out a vial of fluid from his medical bag and prepares to inject her.

Mum manages to sit up. "What's in that bottle?"

Dave is focused on transferring the fluid into the syringe.

He draws it through the needle and gives the syringe a flick with his fingernail. "It's ketamine," he says.

"Ketamine?" Mum frowns. "Dave, that's horse tranquiliser!"

Dave nods. "It's all good, Julia, trust me, it works on humans too. It's good for pain relief."

I think Mum's worried because Dave isn't actually a doctor. But there are no doctors in Parnassus and he's a very good vet. He gave Gus his strangles shot last week. Anyway, once he gives Mum the horse tranquiliser she seems much happier, and she drifts off to sleep as Dave examines the leg and straightens it out and puts sticks on either side of it and wraps it in bandages.

"There's definitely a fracture in the femur," he says to Mrs Mahuta, who's standing and watching him work. "But the worrying thing is the pelvis. It looks like there could be issues there, possibly some internal bleeding. I'll bring in the ultra-sound machine in the morning once she's had some rest, and we'll know more then."

He sees the worried look on my face and gives me a reassuring smile. "Your mum will be fine, Evie."

I know he's trying to be kind, but it makes me want to cry when he's so nice to me. Mrs Mahuta sees me looking all wobbly and tearful and she puts her arm round me. "Come on, hun, let's leave Mum to sleep for a bit now, eh? We'll go and put our tent up."

By now it's four in the morning and people keep turning up and you can hear everyone calling out to each other in the dark. Mayor Garry has drawn a map that explains to everyone where they can set up their tents and stuck it on the wall of the town hall. He's already erected three E-Z Ups and brought out gas barbecues to cook on because there's no power. Also there are no showers and no toilets because the plumbing has stopped working.

"We need some bottles of water and some matches and candles," Mr Mahuta says, sending me and Moana to the dairy. Moana puts out her hand for money.

"I don't have any cash. Tell Scary Mary I'll pay her later."

Moana looks at me. We both know that Scary Mary doesn't give credit – there's a sign above the till that says so in big red letters.

"Oh, and Mo," Mr Mahuta says, "grab some food for us as well, eh?"

"Like what?" Moana says.

"Whatever they've got," Mr Mahuta says. "See if she still has any pies in the warmer."

Moana and I walk down the street together. I'm still

holding Moxy in my arms. I want to let her go, but right now I don't trust her not to run away, so I keep my arms tightly round her.

"Do you think we can get ice creams?" Moana asks me.

"What if Gemma isn't there?" I say. She's the only one who serves decent-size scoops.

Moana shrugs. "Choc Bombs."

We walk past the charity shop. It's closed because it's still the middle of the night but through the windows you can see all the clothes racks have toppled over. There's stuff all over the floor and broken pottery everywhere.

"There's Gemma!"

Gemma has a broom and she's sweeping up broken glass. The whole front window of the dairy has smashed. We pick our way through and I give Gemma a hug. The broom kind of sticks into me and it's a bit awkward and we both laugh.

"Is your mum OK?" Gemma asks.

"She's got a broken leg," I say. "Dave gave her some horse tranquiliser and she's sleeping."

Scary Mary is inside the dairy at the counter. She's got her hands on her hips and she is deep in conversation with Mayor Garry.

Garry Giddens runs the Wrightsons over the road. He thinks he owns Parnassus so everyone calls him 'Mayor Garry' behind his back. He has a feud going with Scary Mary. Everyone knows about it and no one is taking sides but really we all think it's Scary Mary's fault because she accused Mayor Garry of squeezing an avocado too hard and said he bruised it and forced him to pay $4.50, and he was furious and now he won't shop at Scary Mary's any more. He has to go all the way over the Waiau bridge and into Cheviot to the Countdown.

Garry is wearing shorts and gumboots and a bush shirt. Scary Mary is wearing a pink spotty dressing gown and purple furry slippers. Behind her, in the aisles, the food has fallen off the shelves and is strewn all over the floor. Garry is standing by the counter with a big stack of bottled water.

"We need the soft drinks out of the fridges too."

Scary Mary frowns. "And who exactly is paying for it?"

Scary Mary is the most tight-fisted person I have ever met. In all my years of going to her dairy, she has never once given me so much as a free aniseed ball.

"Insurance," Garry says confidently.

"Yeah, like they paid in Christchurch after the big quake

there! There are still people waiting for their money..." Scary Mary stops mid-rant. She gives a sigh of resignation. "Take whatever you need. You want some potato crisps and biscuits for the kids?"

Then Garry bends down to her – Scary Mary is way shorter than him – and he gives her this big hug. Moana and I almost die on the spot! I expect Scary Mary to thump him. Everyone knows she has no time for Garry. But she hugs him right back!

"Tell Sherry to come over when she has time and we'll start organising a cooking roster," Scary Mary says. "That power supply isn't coming back on in a hurry so we need to figure out what to do with the food in the freezers before it goes off. If we're going to be stuck here for a while, we need a game plan to feed everyone."

"What does she mean we're stuck here?" I ask Gemma.

"The Waiau bridge is down between here and Cheviot," Gemma says. "And we can't get out the other way through the Kaikoura road either."

We are trapped in both directions.

***

"Mum, are you awake?"

It's six in the morning. Almost dawn. Mum is lying very still in the camp bed when I get back to her. I crouch down beside her so that I can check she's actually breathing. I can see her chest rising and falling very softly. I want to get into the bed and snuggle in with her like I do sometimes at home, but I can't because I will wake her up. Also, she has that wooden splint on her leg.

"Evie?" I feel a large hand clasp my shoulder and look up to see Mr Mahuta beside me. He puts his finger to his lips telling me to be quiet and gestures for me to follow him out of the tent.

Outside, Moana and Arama are already in the ute.

"We're going to do the milking. You want to come and check on Gus?" he asks.

Milking time was an hour ago. Our cows will be waiting at the gate, their pink udders will be stretched taut from the pressure of the pent-up milk. It's really painful for a cow if they don't get milked on time.

I clamber on board the flatbed of the ute and Moana makes space for me next to her. Jock jumps up too and goes to his favourite spot, perched in the corner by the cab with his paws on the side of the ute. He rides like that with his mouth open to catch the wind, and sometimes he leans so far over it looks like he'll fly off if we hit a bump, but he's never fallen.

We're all on board, and Mr Mahuta is pulling away from the hall, when there's an ear-splitting yowl and Moxy comes sprinting between the tents and across the lawn. She makes this massive leap on to the back and lands on me. I snatch her up and cuddle her in my arms as we drive. Her purr is as loud as the car engine.

"Your cat is crazy," Moana says. She means it in a good way. Moxy's not like normal fraidy cats. She's always been an adventurer. Even as a kitten she would ride on the quad bike with Dad like a working dog. She's always meowing for me today, and I know it's because of what happened last night. Moxy is desperate not to get left behind ever again.

On the radio they keep saying that State Highway One is closed from Seddon – which is way up the coast, north, past Kaikoura – all the way in the other direction, to Cheviot, which is ten minutes to the south of us over the Waiau bridge. The inland path along the Leader Road is still being cleared and no one knows when it will be drivable again, so right now there is no way out of Parnassus.

Now that it's daylight, I can see what the earthquake has done. There are mudslides and fallen rocks on the road, and there's even a bit of farmland where a solid wall has risen up in the middle of the paddock, running in a long seam like the Great Wall of China.

"Ohmygod, Mo, look!" The macrocarpa hedge that used to run as a windbreak along the fenceline of Mayor Garry's farm has been unearthed and wrenched out so that the root bulbs stick up in the air like baby teeth that have all come loose at once.

Mr Mahuta drives straight up to the milking shed. I can see his cows, stomping impatiently at the gate, and in the field beside them is my Gus!

I leap off the back of the ute with Moxy and Jock running alongside me. When he sees the three of us, Gus whinnies his head off! Moxy starts up yowling too, as if she's greeting him back. I forget how tight those two are sometimes. She jumps up on the fence post beside him and smooches against his muzzle. I throw my arms round him and give him a hug.

I'm not leaving him here any longer.

"You can come back into town with us." I slip his bridle on and do up the throat lash and the cavesson and then I lead him back towards the milking shed.

Arama is at the gates, about to let the cows through, when we hear Mr Mahuta shout out from inside the shed. He says a swear word. A really bad one. Then he comes out and shouts at Arama.

"Shut the gates! No point bringing them through. We've got no power."

As if they understand and are heartbroken by the news that the milking is not going to happen, the cows start letting out miserable bellows.

"Can you milk them by hand?" I ask.

Mr Mahuta shakes his head. "Sixty cows by hand? I'd need arms like Superman."

I look at the cows. They look sad. But then cows always do, don't they?

"Arama," Mr Mahuta calls out, "get the quad bike. We'll take them next door to Evie's. There's a generator. We can milk them there."

Arama tries to move the cows with the quad bike, but they just kind of stand there defiantly. They know their routine and they don't want to leave. They want to come in and relieve the pain that's building up in their udders.

"Jock!" I whistle my dog around and he comes up to the herd, his tail held up behind him stiff in the air as he hustles back and forth on his busy paws. "Get around, Jock!" I command as he begins to work back and forth, weaving in front of the cows. They let out bellows of discontent, but they obey and turn round and begin to move.

Me and Gus and Arama on his quad bike herd the cows over the ridge while Mr Mahuta and Moana go on ahead in the ute.

Mr Mahuta needs to muck about for a bit to get the generator working, and then we drive the cows straight into the shed and hook them up to the machines. Then the shed is filled with the hypnotic hum of the milk pumping into the vats.

Mr Mahuta watches the cows as their udders are drained and then sends the next lot through until they are all done.

Mr Mahuta is on the phone while the last cows are milked, and once they're done he says to Arama, "Go and attach the hosepipes from the milk vats to the irrigation system."

Arama is confused. "What for?"

"We're going to spray the fields," Mr Mahuta says.

"What?" Arama looks puzzled. "Why?"

"I just talked to the dairy company and the tankers can't get through until the roads open again. We've got to dump it – dump all of it."

The cows will need milking every day to stop them being in pain and drying off. That's thousands of litres of milk thrown away each day. I watch as the irrigators start to spin and the milk fills the pipes and arcs out from the sprinklers, spreading white droplets in a haze across the sky. And I think how weird life is right now when you can't trust the earth beneath your feet to stay still, and the rain is made of milk.

"Can we go into your house?" Moana wants to see it. She wasn't with us last night when we came back for Mum, and when she sees the wreckage where my house used to be she is astonished. It does look worse in the daylight. I can see bits of our old life poking out from beneath the broken beams. Sofas and tables, a smashed-up TV set. And at the back of the house, there's my bedroom with no walls and no roof, my universe exposed to the sky above.

"All your stuff is in there," Moana says. "We should go in and get your things."

I feel revulsion at the idea. That bedroom held me captive. It was the centre of my OCD universe, the Pandora's box that my rituals sprang from. And now it's destroyed and I'm free and I don't want any of it any more. Not my clothes, my toys, my books, my bed... they're all infected with the OCD. So let it remain beneath the rubble. I don't want to go back.

"Come on!" Moana urges. "Let's go in..."

"You kids!"

It's Mr Mahuta.

"Don't you go near that house! It's not safe. The whole place could collapse beneath you."

So that's final then. I turn my back on the house for the last time. I'm leaving it all behind.

Not quite all. As I ride Gus down the road towards Parnassus, I feel the weight of the backpack on my back. The bedroom has been destroyed, but my portable nest of OCD is still here with me, attached like a limpet, refusing to let me go.

***

Zip-unzip, zip-unzip. Do it again. I unpack the items from my backpack and I do my rituals. I've searched the riverbank for hours and nothing. I was certain we'd find some sign of Moxy. But we can't look any longer. We need to get going. We've been searching half a day and the rescue ship – the HMS *Canterbury* – is on the way, and if we don't carry on, we'll miss it. We're running out of time. We have no choice. And so we turn away, just the three of us, heading up into the hills of the Hundalees.

CHAPTER 9

The Odyssey

By mid-afternoon the skies have darkened, and as Gus and Jock and I make our way up into the foothills of the Hundalees the clouds become black and threatening. There's a storm coming.

Maybe I should have retraced the river to State Highway One, but I thought going back all the way to the road was pointless and this way would be a shortcut. We've lost so much time combing the riverbanks. The HMS *Canterbury* will pull into Kaikoura in two days' time and if we're not there we'll miss the boat. Then all of this – losing Moxy – will have been for nothing.

I wonder if they've realised back in Parnassus that I'm gone?

***

"We're evacuating."

It is the day after the quake and Mayor Garry has gathered everyone from our makeshift tent village into the town hall to make the announcement. We're leaving Parnassus.

"They're going to open the Leader Road inland," Mayor Garry says. "We should be able to leave by car first thing tomorrow morning."

"So we're heading north?" Scary Mary asks. "Where to?"

"Through Mount Lyford to Kaikoura," Mayor Garry says. "They're sending in a warship to dock in Kaikoura harbour to evacuate the coast. It'll arrive in four days."

"A boat?" Mrs Mahuta asks. "Can we take our stuff with us?"

"It's not a cruise ship, Louise," Mayor Garry says. "We can only take essentials. Pack your cars with warm blankets and clothes and food and water, and that's it. No luggage."

"What about the dogs?" Moana asks. Black and Decker,

112

the Mahutas' two big black Labradors, are currently lying at Mr Mahuta's feet, their heads on their paws.

"No animals." Mayor Garry shakes his head.

"What do you mean, no animals?" Mrs Mahuta bristles.

"No pets," Mayor Garry clarifies. "They have to stay behind."

"That's ridiculous!" Mrs Mahuta says. "What are we supposed to do? Just leave the dogs at home with a tin opener and let them fend for themselves? Don't talk nonsense, Garry!"

There's a murmur through the crowd gathered in the hall, and Mayor Garry holds up his hands to calm us all.

"This is an evacuation," Garry says. "Human life takes priority."

"Oh, for God's sake!" Scary Mary rolls her eyes at him. "Stop talking like you run the show, Garry, and actually get off your backside and do something for once! Get on the phone to those blokes at Civil Defence and tell them we're not getting on that boat without our pets!"

"Yeah," Moana says. "And that includes Buffy and Willow!"

Buffy and Willow are Moana's guinea pigs.

Garry stomps out with his phone clutched to his ear and there's a tense silence while we wait for him to talk with the Civil Defence people.

113

When he comes back in, Mayor Garry looks all pleased with himself. "OK," he says, "I've had serious words with Civil Defence. The SPCA is sorting it. Animals will be allowed on board the HMS *Canterbury*, so when you pack the cars, leave room for the pets."

"That's more like it!" Mrs Mahuta says, giving Black and Decker a pat. "You hear that, boys? You're coming with us!"

"They're sending in a helicopter too." Mayor Garry continues. "They'll airlift Julia straight to the hospital in Christchurch."

"Evie," Scary Mary says, "you can go with your mum if you want. We'll take Jock and Moxy with us in the car and meet you there."

"What about Gus?" I say.

"What about him?" Scary Mary is puzzled.

"He won't fit in the car."

There's a silence in the hall.

"Evie," Mayor Garry says, "don't be silly. Gus can't come."

"Why not?" I bristle. "You just said we can take the pets."

"Gus isn't a pet," Mayor Garry says. "He's a farm animal."

I can hear the bees coming into my brain, my blood

114

pounding in my temples. "He's my horse! I can't just leave him alone."

There's a deafening quiet in the room. Then Scary Mary says, "Evie, he won't be alone. You can put him in with the cows for company."

"He doesn't care about cows!" I shout at her. "He needs me and Jock and Moxy!"

None of them know! If they saw what Gus was like that last night during the earthquake they'd understand. There are going to be more aftershocks and he's going to hurt himself.

"Evie," Mayor Garry is speaking to me in that syrupy voice you use when you're trying to convince a little kid about something, like he's tempting me with ice cream and lollies. "Don't you want to go in a helicopter? You can even take Moxy and Jock with you."

As if I care about a stupid helicopter ride! If I have to go without Gus then I'm not going anywhere. I will never ever leave my pony behind.

"Mum?" I come into her tent and she can see straight away I've been crying.

"Evie, what's the matter?"

"Mayor Garry is a moron," I say.

Mum tries to sit up in bed and I see her wince. "We all know that," she says. "What's he done now?"

"He wants me to leave Gus behind and go in the helicopter with you," I say. "But I told him I would never leave Gus alone."

I look at her, expecting support. My mum was a horse rider too, back in the day. She knows how special Gus is to me.

"I do understand that you want to take him with us," she says, "but he's not going to fit in a helicopter, Evie."

"He'll fit on a ship, though."

Mum's face softens. "I know you love him, but Gus is a horse, sweetie. They're used to living outside. He'll be fine at the farm. He's happy in a paddock by himself."

"Not with earthquakes!" I say. "Mum you didn't see him that night when the house fell. He was so scared, he was galloping around like crazy and he could have killed himself. And I promised him! I told him then I'd never leave him alone again!"

"Evie –" Mum looks at me – "don't get hysterical. This is a state of emergency right now, but when the roads are cleared and things are sorted we'll come back for him."

"When?"

"As soon as we can."

"What if it's months?" I say. "What if we can't ever come back? What if the roads are closed forever because of earthquakes..."

"Evie," Mum is actually getting cross with me now. "I can't do anything about this! Even if there was room on the ship, there's no way to get a horse to Kaikoura. You don't have a choice. You have to leave him behind!"

"Then I'm not going either!" I say. "I'll stay here with him and Jock and Moxy."

"You can't do that," Mum says. "There's no water, no food. We don't know how long it will be before we get the power back on. Evie, we've got to leave."

I look at Mum and I realise that this is pointless. She is just like the rest of them. Adults. They say they love animals but really they think people are more important. But they're not.

And at that moment I realise it is up to me. I am the only one who cares enough to save Gus. And that is when I think up my plan – to ride the coast road to Kaikoura and meet the ship with my pony.

And I take a deep breath as if I am admitting defeat and I say, "OK, but I can't go on the helicopter with you because of my OCD..."

I stay by Mum's bedside until the helicopter comes and I feel awful about lying and even more awful about being separated from her, because she is going to *the place*. They are taking her to Christchurch Hospital, and I don't want her to go there because I know what can happen when you follow the red line. I'm worried about Mum, and when she's asleep, before the helicopter comes, I do the rituals with my backpack beside her bed to try to keep her safe. I need to protect her.

Moana comes to get me when the helicopter arrives. It's a black one. It looks like a wasp in the sky as it comes in to land.

The helicopter pilots crouch down low and run out from under the helicopter blades while they're still rotating. I walk alongside while Mayor Garry talks to them. The tall dark-haired one is called Charlie and he's the pilot. The other one, Nathan, has sandy blond hair. He's the one who looks after my mum.

"How are you doing, Mrs Van Zwanenberg?"

Nathan reaches down and picks up her hand, taking her pulse at the wrist. "Can I have a look at that leg?" He moves the sheet off so he can see it.

"Wiggle your toes for me?" Nathan says.

Mum winces as they wiggle.

"That's good," Nathan says. "You've got feeling in them, yeah?"

Mum nods.

"Now, I'm going to put my hand under your foot. Press down on me as hard as you can, OK?"

"Ughh." Mum whimpers a little. Nathan is making notes in his phone.

"OK!" he calls out to Charlie. "She's prepped over here. We're good to go."

Mum gets a panicked look on her face. She grabs tighter on to my hand.

"Are you sure you can't come with me in the helicopter, Evie?" she says. "They could give you some medication to make you calm and then you could fly?"

I shake my head. "I'll be fine, Mum."

"If you need anything, ask Mrs Mahuta, OK?" Mum says.

Nathan smiles at me. "Going in the convoy, huh? Well, you'll catch us up in a few days. Your mum will still be in the hospital, so I guess we'll see you there?"

Suddenly I get this pang in my gut like I've done the wrong thing. And I want to say I will go too. But it's too late because Nathan and Charlie are lifting up Mum's stretcher now and carrying her out of the tent. I run alongside them as they walk out with her to the helicopter. They open the doors and load her stretcher inside and I get in too, crouching beside her.

"Mum?"

I'm scared to hug her in case I hurt her, but I do it anyway. My arms splay round the outside of the red wool emergency blanket she's wrapped in. I burrow my head into her chest and she kisses me on top of my head.

"I'll see you in a few days, Evie," Mum says. "I love you."

"Bye, Mum," I whisper. "I love you too."

But when I say "I love you" Charlie starts the helicopter engine, so I'm not completely sure that Mum even heard me. I shout it again, but it's too late because I have to climb out now, as they shut the doors. Scary Mary has me by the shoulders and she crouches down with me beneath the whirring blades and moves me away so that we are clear and standing back on the lawn with Mayor Garry, who's dressed in a ridiculous orange hi-vis jacket which he took from road patrol. We watch the rotors whirr until they turn invisible. Charlie and Nathan both have their headsets and their sunglasses on and I see Nathan give me a thumbs-up signal through the bubble window of the helicopter windscreen. Then the chopper lifts straight up and into the sky.

Everyone gathers around to watch it leave. Eventually they all go off to pack their cars again, but I stay there alone and watch until the helicopter is no more than a dot. Finally I can't see anything in the sky except blue. Mum is gone.

Then I walk back to the hall and think about what I need to do. It's sixty kilometres to Kaikoura. The warship arrives in four days. I don't have much time.

"What are you doing?"

Moana has walked into the tent and found me packing up.

"I'm going to Kaikoura," I say. "I'm taking Gus."

"What are you talking about?" Moana says. "We can't take him in the station wagon. We've only just got enough room for all of us and the dogs and Moxy."

"I'm not going with you," I say. "I'm going along the coast road."

"But it's shut! You can't get through."

"I can too," I say. "Cars can't get through, but a horse can."

"You're going to ride to Kaikoura?" Moana looks at me and I know that look!

"You have to promise me," I say. "Promise me you won't tell!"

"But when Mum finds out you're gone she'll be really angry," Moana says.

"Say I changed my mind and went in the helicopter with my mum."

"She won't believe me."

"Then make up another lie," I say.

"Like what?"

I pick up my sleeping bag and the pup tent. And then I put them down again and I give Moana a hug. A really tight hug.

"I don't know," I say. "You'll think of something."

Moana frowns. "So you're going to meet us on the other side?"

I nod.

"What if the roads are too bad and you can't get through?"

"I'll make it."

"You'll have to cross the Hundalees."

"I know."

Moana looks worried. "You shouldn't do this."

I look her in the eye. "If Gus was your horse, would you leave him behind?"

"No," she says.

I pick up the sleeping bag and the tent. "Me neither."

***

When my OCD was really at its worst, when the bees in my brain were driving me mad, before I ever told Mum what was wrong with me, I figured out that the only way I could stop the rituals was to do absolutely nothing. And so I'd lie in bed and not move. I'd shut my eyes, because that way the OCD couldn't make me do anything. Only it turned out I couldn't just stay in bed all day because, well, life forces you to do things.

I wish I could have done nothing but stay in Parnassus. I didn't want to do this. But Gus is my best friend. And best friends do not leave each other. I made the choice to try and save Gus. But that's the problem with choices – we never know until it's too late if they've been right or wrong. If I hadn't made the decision to make this journey, Moxy would still be alive right now. My decision, my fault. Everything is always my fault. I've been trying so hard not to cry about Moxy, but I look back at the spot on Gus's rump where she should be sitting and I feel the hot tears stinging my cheeks and I wish I could talk to Willard Fox right now.

I thought we would be able to get through this way from Conway Flat to the Hundalees, but the hills in front of us are too steep and the scree on the surface is loose, so I worry that if we try to go straight up we'll end up starting a rockslide. Or if there's another aftershock when we are halfway up then we'll get buried alive.

So I give up on the path we've taken and I go back the way we came along the riverbank until we're at State Highway One again. It seems so quiet now without Moxy. She was a very loud cat. And even when she wasn't talking her presence filled the space around you, like she had a way of making herself involved.

I should have brought a raincoat with me. I didn't even think about that when I left. Now, just as we reach the highway again, the rain begins to fall and I hear the thunder from the clouds above us. *Zeus is angry, Willard Fox. I can hear him.*

By the time we've reached the signpost for the Hundalees, I'm soaked to the skin for the second time today. All my stuff is wet too and it's getting dark.

As we round a corner, I see a one-eyed giant in the middle of the road looming up at me. I freeze and hope that I haven't been seen, because this was the last thing I was expecting. How did I not hear it? The rumble of the thunder must have drowned it out, but now it's too late. The glassy eye bears down on me and I have nowhere to escape to. I am in the path of the Cyclops.

CHAPTER 10

Helen of the Hundalees

The glassy-eyed Cyclops rumbles round the bend in the road in front of us. It's a giant earthmover. I feel the tremors as it shakes the ground beneath us, as turbulent as an aftershock.

I think we've been seen and hold my breath, but then the Cyclops reverses and begins to go backwards, retreating along the same stretch of road. We need to get out of the way now, because next time we might not be so lucky!

"Gus!" He's frozen with fear in front of the massive earthmover, but I give him a vigorous kick and that wakes him up. With Jock at his heels I ride to the shoulder of the road and straight off the edge, careening down the steep bank that leads into the trees beyond.

Hidden by the trees, sheltered from the rain, I pull Gus back round so that we're facing the road and peering back out through the low-hanging branches. The earthmover really does look like a Cyclops, the gigantic glass bubble-eye cab containing the driver, like a tiny Lego man at the controls.

Behind the gigantic earthmover I can see the rest of the road crew – a couple of other smaller earthmovers and a ute and a landcruiser parked to one side, and half a dozen men in fluorescent vests calling each other on walkie-talkies and setting up road cones. They are moving away a mudslide that covers the whole of the highway and the Cyclops is working back and forth, shifting the mud and giant boulders.

I knew that eventually I would be bound to run into a road crew. I've thought about this moment, about how they would react. If State Highway One is closed to all cars, I figure it's a pretty certain bet that they're not going to make an exception for a twelve-year-old travelling on a pony – even if Gus is a better off-road vehicle than any of their four-wheel drives. If they see us, they'll have no choice. They'll make us turn round and escort us home.

I'm sure the man driving the Cyclops didn't see me and Gus and Jock, or he'd already be telling the others and they'd be hunting for me. So I'm safe. They don't know we're here.

I stay there beneath the trees, bent down over Gus's shoulder, and watch the Cyclops working back and forth, scooping the dirt away, piling it up in a great heap on the side of the road, then reversing and beginning the process all over again.

The rain is getting heavier now. Maybe the weather will make the men decide to pack up their things and leave. But I doubt it. They're all in heavy raincoats and brimmed hats to keep off the weather. As the rain begins to fall even harder, I see the steam coming off the engines and I hear the roar of the diggers and I know I don't have a choice. We can't go back to the highway now, we must stick to the trees, stay in the woods where the ground is rough and hilly. It will take us twice as long to get through, but at least we'll be safe here and they won't find us and...

Jock!

What's he doing? He's back out on the road! He's running towards the road crew.

"Jock!" I hiss at him from my hiding place in the trees.

Argh! That's the problem with Border collies – they're too friendly. Jock's the sort of dog who likes to be everyone's pal. I should have realised and kept an eye on him! He's going to give us all away by racing up to the road workers and introducing himself, like he always does to strangers. He thinks he's being friendly by offering himself up for pats. This time, though, his cheerful greeting is not harmless at all. If the road crew see him, he's going to lead them straight to me and Gus!

"Jock!" He can't hear my voice above the roar of the engines. "Jock!"

He's in the middle of the road. Any minute now one of them is going to notice him.

"Jock!" I shout again, and when it doesn't work this time I put my fingers in my mouth like my dad taught me to do and I give the farm dog whistle.

It's loud and piercing, even through the roar of

the engines, and it stops Jock dead in his tracks. He turns round and looks at me, and when I whistle again he begins to sprint back to me. I watch him run and I hold my breath, hoping that I got him in time, that he'll make it to the trees before they turn and see him.

"Jock! Ohmygod!" I reach out and grab him back into the bushes. Did they see him? I hold my breath for a moment, clutching my dog to me.

I can't believe we got away with it! Nobody saw him.

I can feel Jock straining at the collar even now, like he wants to run back out there again.

"No! Jock!" I speak firmly to him, because I know I need to be tough about this. "You have to stay with me," I tell him. "Heel, Jock, heel. OK?" Backing me up, Gus puts his ears back and shakes his head at Jock too, as if to say, *Yeah, toe the line!*

Jock stays at heel after that. Even on the steep bits of the hills where he would usually pick his own track and run across and down the banks, he stays close. I think he's taking me literally. I had only planned to go off-road for long enough to circle around the road crew, but now that I'm in the trees I can see that there's a gorge between me and the next ridge. If I'd stuck to the road, it would have cut through the hills, but now that I'm in the trees I have no choice but to detour round further away still and then up the other side where the conifers are dense on the mountains of the Hundalees. I'm pretty sure if I can get to the top of the ridge on that side then I'll be able to ride back to the road again from there.

The rain is really heavy now, and it's closing in with no sign of letting up for the night. The trees protect us from the worst of it, but I'm still getting wet. I think about unpacking the sleeping bag and wrapping myself in that, but it would be hard to ride wrapped up like a puffball so I leave it, and by the time we reach the ridge, I'm soaked to the skin.

There's nowhere good here to pitch the tent, so even though it's getting dark now I think I should just keep riding on. I'm kicking myself a little, because maybe if I'd just stayed crouched in the bushes and waited, the road crew would have packed up and gone home. I could have ridden straight through and I wouldn't be stuck out here on this ridge. But then I think of the slip covering the road and how one good aftershock would probably send the whole cliff face tumbling down on top of the tarmac, and I think I would rather be here, high up in the hills with the trees to protect me, than on that road where another mudslide could swamp me alive.

At the top of the ridge I can see there's a path that leads up through the forestry, further into the depths of the Hundalees, and I'm pretty sure if I take this path I will get to the other side of the mountains and rejoin the road eventually, so I press on.

It is getting so dark now, it'll be hard to pitch the tent, but then again it's too wet to sleep rough. I need shelter. I find a flat area beneath a conifer tree, reasonably dry too, and I'm just about to dismount and unpack my gear when Jock gives a deep, throaty growl and charges forward.

"Jock!" What is it this time?

I cluck Gus on and follow after him, afraid that as the night is falling, if we lose Jock now then we'll never find him again. We crest the top of the ridge then head down the other side through trees, and then there's a clearing up ahead. Jock is waiting there, on the doorstep of a house.

There is a house, here in the middle of nowhere. Black creosoted wood, and a green front door with faded, peeling paint. It almost blends in with the woods around it, the colours of the trees. It has two front windows and a door and a doorstep too, where Jock is now sitting and waiting for me, sheltered from the rain that is getting harder.

There are no lights on inside.

"Hello?" I call out.

Nothing. Jock runs back from the door to greet me as I dismount from Gus and lead him closer. There's a tree with low-hanging branches so I tie the reins across a branch and walk up to the front of the house. The curtains on the windows are closed. I can't see in. I walk up to the front door and knock hard.

"Hello?" I call out.

No reply. I try the handle. It opens and the door swings. But it stops and jams about halfway open and I can see why. The narrow hallway ahead of me has dark floorboards and gloomy wallpaper. It's crammed with newspapers and magazines. They sit in piles stacked as high as my head, yellowed and dog-eared – the *Kaikoura Star*, ancient copies of *Good Housekeeping* and *Fishing and Hunting* magazine, and next to that, a mouldering pile of *Horse & Pony*. The piles are covered in dust so thick it looks like icing on cakes. I have to wind my way between the stacks, turning my body sideways just to fit up the hall.

"Hello?" I call again. Still nothing. "Is anyone home? Your door was open and I let myself in…"

Out of the corner of my eye I see a shadow flicker on the wall and I turn round, heart pounding, but it's just the trees outside moving, their silhouettes reflected in the dying evening light. I keep walking down the hall, and now I can see what I think is the kitchen at the far end. As I walk, I catch glimpses through the open doorways that split off from the hall, and in all the rooms are more of the same: piles of dusty magazines and newspapers, and other items in teetering stacks of boxes. Cardboard cartons of empty bottles and dusty glass jars filled with strange liquids. Soft toys and suitcases overspilling with knitted jumpers. All of it is crammed into the usable space of the rooms so that the actual furniture – beaten-up old sofas, creaky beds and wooden tables and chairs – is virtually hidden from view.

It's creepy here, but familiar too in a strange way, and as I walk I get this sudden flashback to my bedroom in Parnassus. This house is my room. On a grander scale, with a centuries-old, dense layer of dust, perhaps, but the matrix, the DNA is the same. The piles in the hallway are chaotic, but strictly organised too. This house didn't end up like this by mistake. Somebody made it this way.

As I get closer to the kitchen, I'm struck by the stench of the place. The old newspapers and magazines have a dank, mildew smell to them, but it's more than that. There's the smell of grease and coal, the whiff of filth, and it grows more intense as I get nearer. When I enter the kitchen I gag a little, because it's not just untidy in here – it's gross! There are no windows, and I'm grateful for the lack of light because I can tell by the smell in here that it's been a long time since somebody bothered to clean. There's a small wooden table, again stacked with old magazines, and a single chair. In one corner there is an old coal range, the sort that they used to cook on in the olden days, stoking a fire inside it to cook the food on top, and it's the coal range that really holds my attention now, because I've just realised something. It's warm.

The door of the range is open and I can see the glowing embers of the coal inside it. Someone lives here! There's a pot on top of the stove and I take the lid off. Whatever is in there smells kind of good in an overcooked way. I can make out vegetables and meat in a brownish sauce, all bubbling away. And now I'm looking around this crazy room, because I know someone has to be here. I can hear the fear in my voice when I call again and say, "Hello? I know you're home. Hello?"

A scuttling noise, like a rat running across the rafters in the stables, comes from the hall. I see the hackles go up on the back of Jock's neck and I feel the hairs rise up on my own. I'm not calling out any more, and I'm not moving any closer. I'm frozen to the spot, heart pounding. Someone else, or something else, is in this house.

The floorboards creak. Footsteps? Someone moving around? Beside me, Jock starts up with a low throaty growl, and I put my hand out to touch the ruff of his neck, more glad than ever that I have him with me.

Footsteps, coming closer, treading up the hall. Jock's growl deepens and my heart is racing so hard now, I can't breathe.

And then, in the kitchen doorway, the shadow emerges. The figure in front of me is so tiny, at first I think she's a child, but then she steps into the kitchen and I see her face, the wrinkles and the grey hair, the hollowed, sunken eyes, and I realise she's not young at all but very, very old.

"Is that an Arab outside?" she asks me.

I don't know what she's asking at first, and then I realise she means Gus.

"My pony?" I say. "Yeah, he's an Arab."

"Thought so." She grunts with satisfaction.

She shuffles closer to me, the same tiny footsteps that I heard coming for me up the hall. She has a walking cane and she barely raises her feet as she moves. She seems to scuff across the floor instead.

I think she's coming towards me but she changes course and goes to the pot on top of the coal range.

"I've made stew," she says. "It's wood pigeon. Killed it myself."

I nod, not sure what to say. I'm pretty sure wood pigeons are endangered, but this doesn't seem like the right time to bring that up.

She doesn't actually ask me if I want any, but she gets two bowls down off one of her filthy shelves, then digs around in a manky drawer. She pulls out a fork and a spoon and considers. She considers her options and eventually gives me the fork. It's crusted with something yellow. Then she uses the spoon to dish us both up a bowlful of the stew and she gestures for me to take the sole seat at the table. She sits herself down on top of the only clear bit of bench space, next to a pile of old newspapers and some more dirty dishes that look like they last got washed a year ago.

"Who are your people?"

Her questions aren't the sort normal people ask. I am Pakeha not Maori, so it's not like I have a tribe or anything.

"My name is Evie. Evie Van Zwanenberg," I say.

"Never heard of you," she says, not bothering to stop eating as she speaks, scoffing down great mouthfuls of the stew.

The rest of our conversation is just as strange and by the end of it she still hasn't given me her name. Although she has told me that I can stay the night, meticulously moving a mountain of newspapers off the sofa so that I can put my sleeping bag there. She will, incredibly, produce a bale of hay for Gus, and a curious-looking meat bone for Jock. She'll stoke the fire in the coal range on a regular basis all the while, refusing to let the coals go out, and she'll fuss about in the dark, lighting strategically located candles that make me think the whole place is going to go up in flames at any moment because the candles are right beside the endless stacks of newspapers, and what if a really big aftershock knocks one over? This place would be an inferno, a death trap. But I don't say anything because I can see that the old woman has her routines. Her rituals. Only when I'm lying down on the sofa, thawing out beneath the warmth of my sleeping bag, and arranging the contents of my backpack – unzip-zip-unzip-zip – do I wonder if she might be crazy and murder me in my sleep, but I'm so exhausted and grateful for the softness of the cushions underneath me that I banish the thought and decide she's just a bit loopy and not dangerous. I still don't know her name, but she will tell me in the morning, when it is light and I can see just how filthy the sofa beneath me is, that it's Helen. Helen of the Hundalees.

CHAPTER 11

The Riddle of the Sphinx

We have wood pigeon stew for breakfast and I offer to do the dishes, but Helen says no and just stacks them on top of the bench where they were before. I don't think those dishes have ever seen a hot tap and soap, and I think about what Willard Fox said to me that first day we met, about how OCD doesn't always mean you like to be clean.

She's not so scary this morning. I watch the way she shambles about the house, fetching me the stew. I see her quiet rituals. The way she always has to walk in a certain direction round the table, making a certain number of clacks with her cane against the furniture. When I'm walking down the hall and

141

my backpack accidentally nudges over a pile of newspapers she comes almost running to fix the stack and mutters rhyming words to herself, nodding her head as she rearranges them so that they're back in position exactly as they were before. I realise it was a big thing for her last night to let me sit in her chair, and probably an even huger thing for her to move those newspapers so that I had somewhere to sleep, and I'm grateful.

In the hallway, with Helen walking behind me, I pause next to the stacks of newspapers, and look at the dusty pile of *Horse & Pony* magazines. I reach out to pick one up and then I see the look on Helen's face and I stop myself. I glance down at the magazine, its cover faded by age, and I read the date on the top corner. It's from 1972.

"Did you have a horse?" I ask Helen.

"Of course," she laughs as if I should know this. "More than one."

"Did you compete?"

Helen looks serious. "I remember, I would get so nervous the night before a competition, I couldn't sleep."

"I get nervous in the start box," I say, "but once I'm out on that cross-country course with my horse, it's like my mind is clear and I'm totally focused. It's the best feeling in the world."

Helen steps up beside me and looks down at the magazine stack, at the picture on the front cover of the magazine sitting on the top. It's a girl on a black horse jumping a massive show jump. Her eyes are looking to the left, so it's clear that she's already focused on the next fence, and the horse is tucking his feet up neatly, and she's wearing a velvet hard hat and a hairnet and white gloves. They look very professional.

"I loved to ride," Helen says wistfully. "Horses are good for making the bees go quiet."

The bees? Did she really just say that?

A pained expression passes over her face and Helen briskly shakes her head as if she's rearranging the jumble of thoughts inside. I know the conversation is over. "I have hay in the shed," she says, heading for the back door. "Pegasus will be needing his breakfast."

That's what she calls Gus. The weird thing is, I don't recall ever telling Helen his real name.

"Pegasus, the winged horse from Parnassus," she coos as she watches Gus devour the hay. When he's down to the last scraps of the hay biscuit, she gathers the scattered remains up off the ground for him and feeds him by hand. I can see her relishing the feeling of his velvety lips against her palm with the joy of a small child. Then once it's all gone, Helen strokes his muzzle and lowers her own head to meet his and whispers, "Where are your thunderbolts now, Pegasus? Have you used them all up or are there more to come? Will you rock the earth again or is your work done?"

This is how she speaks. Like everything is a riddle. She reminds me of the Sphinx in the Greek myths. The Sphinx would stop travellers on the road and ask them a riddle, and if they got the answer right they would be allowed to live, but if they got it wrong the sphinx would eat them. It was always the same question and no one ever got it right until this guy Oedipus, so everyone got eaten, I guess. And the riddle was this:

What creature has four legs in the morning, two legs at midday and three legs in the evening?

The answer is: man. We crawl on all fours as a baby, walk upright on two legs when we grow up, and then when we're old, like Helen, we use a walking stick as our extra leg to make three.

I don't know how old Helen is. I asked her how long she'd been living here in this house and who built it.

"It's my house," she said. "I've been here since the start, I was here when the trees were saplings." Which sounds impressive but what does it actually mean? And anyway, this is forestry land so surely some of these trees here are young, younger than me even, let alone ancient old Helen?

"I'm twelve," I tell her, even though she hasn't asked. She never asks me anything normal. "I'm going to Kaikoura. There's a boat coming and I'm going to evacuate with the others."

"Kaikoura," Helen shakes her head. "Glittering city on the sea." I don't know what she's talking about because Kaikoura isn't a city, it's got like maybe a couple of thousand people and even fewer when the tourist season isn't happening.

"Do you ever go into Kaikoura? For food, and

145

stuff?" I ask. The shops there must be the nearest to the Hundalees.

"Oh no!" Helen shakes her head vigorously. "I don't need the shops. I kill what I eat." And she raises her hands and extends her left arm and draws the right one back, miming a hunter drawing taut the string on a bow and letting loose the arrow.

"What do you kill?" I ask, thinking of the wood pigeon in her pot and wondering what other endangered species might be getting culled and cooked up by this frail little old woman.

Helen's eyes go wide at this question as if she is remembering something very exciting. "Yesterday," she says, "I shot a leopard."

OK, now she's officially crossed the border to crazy town. This is New Zealand – there are no wild cats here. Certainly there are no leopards roaming the hills of the Hundalees.

"What did it look like?"

"It was this big…" Helen spreads her arms out wide then slowly brings her hands closer together, so that she's holding them the length of a bread loaf apart. It's as if she's describing a fish she's caught, and it has just shrunk from a marlin to a trout.

"A leopard with a serpent's tail."

And I don't know why, but I know straight away, without a doubt, who she's talking about.

"Moxy!" I say. "Was it a cat? A dark brown cat?"

"Noooo," Helen is adamant. "Not a cat! Funny-looking creature. A leopard, but small, with no fur."

"That's her!" I say. "That's my cat!"

And then I think of the pot of stew on the stove. Did I just eat my own cat for dinner last night? Was that Moxy, or was that wood pigeon? I'm almost scared to ask the next question.

"Did you kill her?"

Helen looks at me, clearly insulted. "I am a very good huntress. I don't miss."

I feel sick with despair until she says, "I saw the arrow fly clean from my bow, but the little leopard was swift and when I hunted in the bushes my arrow was there, held firm in the wood of a tree."

So maybe she did miss! Moxy might still be alive.

***

I saddle up Gus as fast as I can after that. I'm trying to think like Moxy. Where would she be now? She's a smart cat and she won't have hung around after the near miss with the bow and arrow. Helen says she was running in the direction of the Stag and Spey – so that's the way we will go from here.

I'm tying the sleeping bag and the tent behind the saddle when the aftershock hits. Jock senses its surge before I do and suddenly starts up barking, and then I hear the boom and a moment later the train-rumble beneath my feet. I look down and see the pine needles dancing, bouncing around like Mexican jumping beans. It's as if the earth below is trying to shrug the rug off its back. Then the trembling becomes more intense, a proper shaking, and I lose my balance and fall against Gus and cling to him.

I stay there with my arms round his neck, holding on. The rumble is strong this time, it shakes us back and forth and up and down at the same time. It reminds me of that time we went to Auckland and Dad and I went on the rollercoaster, the way the force of the turns pressed us hard back into our seats and then loosed us again so that we were compressed upwards into the straps of our harnesses. Only there's no harness to hold me here and I'm struggling against the ground to stay upright.

And then it's over. I stand there and cling to Gus for a long time, breathing hard, waiting for the huge adrenalin surge that's filling my system to normalise a little. When truly deep primal fear strikes you, it's as if all your senses become more awake, and at that moment as I hold on to Gus I can smell the sweetness of him, that horsey smell that all my life has felt like home to me. It soothes me more than any ritual could do. It keeps the bees quiet. I realise at this moment that all this time I thought I was saving Gus by bringing him with me, but I didn't admit to myself that I needed him too. Long before the earthquake, my world was already falling apart. And through it all, my father's death and my OCD, I have had my arms round Gus every day, and he has held me upright, my own two legs combining with his four legs to become pillars of strength together. At my worst moments, Gus and I have been as one. We stand together on six legs. The sphinx has a new answer to her riddle.

When I finally feel like the earth has definitely stopped moving and it's safe, I let Gus go. I tie his reins to the rope attached to the tree and I go back inside the house.

"Helen?" I can't see her at first but I can hear her in the gloom at the kitchen end of the hallway, muttering dark incantations. She's behind a stack of magazines on her hands and knees, repiling the copies of *Horse & Pony* that have been knocked into a state of shambles by the aftershock.

I come to join her and bend down to help, but she turns and snarls at me like a wild animal.

"Don't touch!" she growls.

I leap back. I can feel the anxiety radiating off her. She's changed completely and the gentleness is gone from her. Is this how I am when my anxiety grips me?

I wait until she has the stack back together. She's fussing with it, turning the magazines over and restacking them, not satisfied, until the complex matrix of her OCD is restored and they are precisely the way they need to be. I can almost hear the bees in her brain from here, they're so loud.

I stand there in the dark of the hall, and I feel sick. I can't just leave her in this house alone like this.

"Helen?" I say. "Why don't you come with me to Kaikoura? You can come on the boat and evacuate with us, come to Christchurch…"

Helen doesn't look up from the floor. I see her body stiffen. "Have to stay here." She carries on stacking the magazines. "Too loud out there. Too shiny, too many bees…"

She looks distressed and I know I'm upsetting her with all this talk of leaving so I let it go.

Helen fusses with the magazines some more and then she looks up at me. "You stay. Stay with me, Evie? I'll teach you to be a huntress…" She looks up at me with haunted eyes. "Teach you how to be safe."

In this moment I can see my fate. I can see myself as Helen, allowing my fears to trap me as hers did in a house like this, to grow and multiply gradually, day by day, until one morning you wake up and you simply think, *I cannot leave this place.* And then you are there for good, like a Greek hero in a myth where he's forever pushing a boulder up a hill, or drinking water but cannot slake his thirst.

And I think of Willard Fox and what he did for me.

If Helen of the Hundalees had been to see Willard Fox when she was twelve, I don't think she'd be stuck here in this madhouse with the newspapers stacked almost to the ceiling and the smell of mildew and coal smoke. No one ever gave her the weapons to fight back. But Willard gave them to me, and I'm using them. I'm not going to be trapped forever.

When my bedroom got destroyed by the earthquake, most of the symbols of my OCD were demolished too. I've been letting go more and more each day, but Willard Fox was right. It's like rust. And I still have a little bit of the rust with me. I strap it on to my back each day. Unzip and zip, unzip and zip. Pen, takeaway container, glasses and notebook. I feel the pull of my rituals as if they're magnets and I am iron. They don't want me to let them go.

I don't want to let go either. That's the thing – I truly wasn't strong enough at first, even when I left Willard Fox's rooms that day. But this journey has made me strong, and Willard Fox is right. My powers are real now. Not the way they were before when I thought I could bring earthquakes and ruin the world. I am not a god. But I am me. I am Evie Violet Van Zwanenberg and I can do this. *I'm in charge, OCD. I'm taking the reins.*

I wait until Helen has sorted the pile and gone back to the kitchen before I pick up my backpack. I don't want her to see what I'm about to do because the last thing I want is to upset Helen by unbalancing her universe. This is about me and she doesn't need to know.

In the spare room where she's stacked the old newspapers back up on the sofa again, I look around for the perfect hiding place. I have to lift down two boxes of glass jars until I find a box with enough space to squeeze the backpack inside right at the very bottom of a stack. I bundle it up tight and stuff it in and then I restack the boxes where they were before, arranging them so precisely – I have experience in these matters – that I am certain Helen will never suspect it is there.

As I walk out of the room I cast one last glance behind me. Then I take a deep breath and I let it go.

It's buried there forever now, my backpack and its contents, like a hidden treasure in a dusty tomb. I won't be going back for it. I don't need it any more.

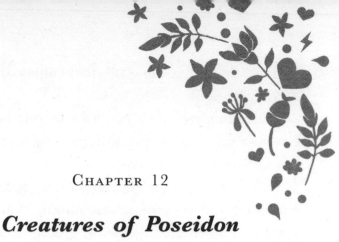

CHAPTER 12

Creatures of Poseidon

We ride all day. That indentation at the top of Gus's rump where Moxy once rode remains empty. Sometimes I turn round and expect to see her sitting there, my most inquisitive companion, her eyes focused on the trees, looking for birds. Each of us go through our lives like that – looking for the things that matter to us, failing to see things that are really there.

I see more now than I did before. The journey has made my senses keen. At nightfall we've made it to the Stag and Spey and as I set up camp I hear nature settling into its nocturnal cadences, the haunting call of the morepork, the rattle of the cicadas, the soft rustling of the hedgehogs on their evening hunt.

My senses still do not extend as far as Jock's however. My dog is the fail-safe – he knows when the aftershocks are coming. My canine alarm system. When he growls out that tremulous bark, I know it will only be a few moments before the "boom" comes and the ground begins to shake. Gus senses the rumbles too. I've seen how his nostrils go wide seconds before they strike. He'll inhale the air with a ragged snort, his ears pricked and tail raised, and for that moment he'll look like a magnificent Arabian stallion and not at all like a 14.2 pony from Parnassus.

I am anxious to leave as soon as it's dawn. The ship arrives in Kaikoura tomorrow and we still have miles to cover, our band of three. I snuggle down in my sleeping bag with Jock pressed up against my side. He's a big dog, but I've realised now that it was Moxy who somehow took up the most room, always squashed up beside my chin, burrowing in for warmth, purring her heart out. We found no sign of her as we left the forests of the Hundalees. Every time I heard a rustling in the trees I hoped it was her. Now, I've realised that our chances of finding her before Kaikoura are like a needle in a haystack. Still, I haven't given up hope that she's alive. She could survive as a wild cat, I guess. She's resourceful and a good hunter. She doesn't need me to put biscuits in her bowl and although I try not to think about the fact that I'll never see her again, in the back of my mind it makes me feel better to know that of all my animals, she's the one who can most take care of herself out there alone.

When I open the tent flap at daybreak the sky is dark blue tinged with soft pink. Red morning, sailors' warning. The rain that struck us in the Hundalees still hangs over the mountains behind us, but when I look in the direction we're going, towards the sea, the sky is clear.

From the Stag and Spey to the coast would take us half the day if we walked steadily, but I'm worried about missing the boat. I don't know what time it arrives or how quickly it will leave again.

As soon as the grassy verges at the side of the

157

road are wide enough and even enough underfoot, I urge Gus into a canter. It's like sitting astride a rocking horse the way he moves, lilting and gentle. Gus never seems to tire. His Arab blood was made for such long journeys, refined over the centuries across the barren desert terrain. He's a descendant of the nomadic mares of Al Khamseh. Distance is his birthright.

We're cantering along the verge when I see a fallen poplar tree up ahead. In a rush of blood, I don't slow Gus down to go round it, I put my legs on and I ride him onwards. Gus sees the tree too, and when he realises my intentions his ears prick. We come in on a strong forward stride and he picks his feet up neatly. We clear it and canter on. And despite his tiredness Gus shakes his head, trying to loosen the reins and take the bit and run. I look for something else, another fallen tree, a ditch, anything we can jump. There's a cattle ramp to the side of the road ahead and we canter up that and then jump down the other side. Jock follows and jumps too. For an old dog, he keeps pace pretty well, tongue lolling happily out, paws moving swiftly at twice the speed of Gus's strides to stick with us. I worry that the speed I'm setting now will exhaust him, but then at one point my dog spies a rabbit in a nearby field and bolts after it until he's just a black and white speck in the distance. If he has the energy to work up enough bloodlust for a hunt, then he's fit enough to make it to the coast at my pony's heels.

When we cross the last ridge we look down to the coast and finally I glimpse the sparkling blue of the sea in the far distance. I feel my heart surge – Kaikoura! I think of Helen and her "glittering city" and at that moment it is shining in front of me. Today the ship will come into port in South Bay to pick up the evacuees. This is what we've made the journey for. So I keep cantering on the downhill roads, but all the time I'm aware of the tiny feline shadow over my shoulder, the vacant space where Moxy once sat up here behind me.

We're back on State Highway One now as we head down to the coast. I haven't seen a road crew since the Cyclops but I know they must have been here working because there are signs of mudslides being cleared to make the roads usable again, and at one point we cross a bridge that didn't even exist before – a makeshift structure of wooden planks that has been built right alongside the original bridge, which is warped and twisted beyond repair. Gus's hooves make a noisy clatter on the planked wood and he startles and spooks at his own hoof beats as they echo back at him. I laugh a little because he's such an Arabian – so brave, but always on tiptoes, always expecting the wild lion who might leap out to eat him!

I can't see the sea any more at this point. The road is winding between sheer man-made cliffs cut into the clay, and I think about the mudslides that have already been cleared from the roads we've passed through. I can't wait to get out the other side because I feel like one good aftershock would bring it all tumbling down around me.

As I feel my heart racing at this thought, I think of my rituals and my backpack, buried deep in the house at the Hundalees, and I look down at Gus's wither where the two braids used to be. I didn't plait his mane this morning. I tell myself that I'm OK, and strangely, I know that I am. We are close now. I can smell the sea. We are getting nearer to Kaikoura.

***

The road crew man holding the stop sign watches me approach and I can see he's wondering what I'm doing out here with my horse and my dog. He's wearing a fluorescent jacket and beneath his broad-brimmed hat, he's poked his T-shirt up at the back to shield his neck from the sun.

"Where'd you come from?" He frowns at me.

"Over the hill back there." I act casual.

"You can't get through here."

"Why not?"

"Road's blocked. There's a slip."

I can't see behind his sunglasses so I don't know what he's thinking. Is he going to send me back?

Then he lowers the sign and points down the road. "You see that dirt track? You take that. It'll lead you down to the beach. Get through that way."

He steps aside with his sign and then gestures for me to walk between the road cones and I continue on my way, down the dirt track to the sea.

I know this beach because we've been here almost every summer since I was born. There's a holiday camp further along at Peketa, where you can pitch tents or rent a cabin, but we've always liked it better here in Oaro, where there are almost no people ever. Except now the beach at Oaro is different, and I can't figure out why at first, but then I realise it's because the sea is so very far away from where it used to be and there are these giant stone pillars that I've never seen before rising up in front of me on the beach. They're covered in paua, which are really big shellfish like mussels, only giant with shiny rainbow-coloured shells. They cling like jewels to the rocks.

I've never seen paua like this before. They normally live deep under the sea and you have to dive to get them. How did they get on to these tall rocks all the way up the beach?

Then I realise – the paua haven't moved at all. They're exactly where they've always been. It's the seabed that's moved! The earthquake has thrust up the entire reef so that it's no longer underwater.

The rocks further down the beach are covered with more paua, and a dozen people are climbing up high and gathering the shellfish into hessian sacks. Paua are really expensive! Sometimes Mum lets me have one fritter at the takeaway in Cheviot. I can't believe they're stealing them, because it's totally illegal to poach them off the rocks!

There's something weird about the way they're gathering them. Usually you'd just prise the shells off with a fish knife. These people, though, they're treating them like delicate bone china.

"Be careful!" a man in a woollen beanie with a big beard calls out across the pillars. "Whatever you do, don't damage the underside beneath the shell!"

He climbs down the rocks with a full sack of paua and wades out into the sea so that he's standing waist-deep in the waves. I can't figure out what he's doing, but then suddenly I see a diver break the surface right in front of him. It's a woman in full scuba gear. Still wearing her dive mask, she takes the sack of paua from him and gives him a thumbs-up signal before she submerges again beneath the waves.

Then another diver surfaces and more sacks are handed over. These people aren't taking the paua, they're relocating them, moving them back into the deep water beyond the new tide mark the earthquake has created.

In the heat of the midday sun I can smell the scent of the shellfish beginning to bake, their shells exposed to the air on the salty reef. The clock is ticking for them as much as it is for me. They have to get the paua back into deep water soon or they'll die.

Jock is on the rocks with them now, making friends, running around and introducing himself to everyone with his tail wagging. *Hello, hello! I'm Jock...*

I'm watching the divers and then the next minute I turn and look for Jock again and I realise he's gone!

I look down the bay and there he is – way, way off in the distance. A black and white speck bolting along the line where the waves meet the shore. What is he doing?

"Jock!"

I call him but he's too far away to even hear my voice. And so I cluck Gus into a canter and I set off after him.

He's moving fast ahead of us, and I sense by his speed that he's on the scent of prey. He's running the same way he does when he's put up a rabbit. There are no rabbits on the beach, though, so maybe it's the gaggle of seagulls on the shoreline that's drawn him?

And then I get a sickening knot in my belly, because I can see it's not the gulls that are the target. There's a rocky promontory sticking out from the beach into the sea where the cove curves up ahead, and sitting on the rocks at the very tip of that reef, basking in the sun, is a sea lion.

Not a little lion pup, but a massive, fully grown adult. He's huge. At least twice the size of Jock. He faces out to sea, lazing on his belly, oblivious to my dog who is bearing down on him at top speed.

The sea lion turns and I see his face, the enormous, soft, doe-brown eyes and whiskery muzzle. He looks angelic, but I know better. I've seen a sea lion at Marine World rip a fish apart with his rows of long, razor-sharp teeth.

"Jock!" I yell into the wind after him. "No!"

He doesn't hear me. As he reaches the reef he

slows down to find his way across the sharp rocks on his tender paws, and I pull Gus up so that I can put my fingers in my mouth and whistle to him. Surely he heard that?

Jock doesn't even turn to acknowledge me! I can't decide if it's because the sea wind is drowning out my whistle, or whether the bloodlust in him is now so strong he's ignoring me.

When I reach the rocks, I fling myself down from Gus's back and run. The soles of my jodhpur boots make me slip and lose my footing. I keep my eyes on my feet, panting and scrambling, and when I look up again I see that I'm too late. Jock has reached the sea lion.

The sea lion stands like a statue on the rocks, the white froth of the surf splashing up and over him. At the sight of the barking Border collie he recoils and raises himself to his full height as he faces him. They are like two prizefighters, assessing their first move. And then, Jock lunges.

He throws himself forward with his jaws open and for a moment I think the sea lion is going to retreat and fling himself into the sea. Instead, he rears up and comes straight back at Jock, and grasps him in his jaws and throws my dog like a ragdoll through the air. Jock gives a startled yelp as he goes flying, and then begins baying in pain as he crashes down hard against the rocks. The sea lion is moving in for the kill. He's remarkably fast on his flippers, lumbering towards my cowering dog. Jock knows he's outmatched, and he's crying like I've never heard him do before, yelping with pain and fear. The sea lion closes in on him and uses his jaws again, holding Jock with his flippers this time as the teeth like long needles sink into the black and white fur of his ruff.

"Get off him! Let him go!" As I run I'm thinking about what I can arm myself with, but there's nothing out here! Not even a piece of driftwood or a stone to use as a weapon.

Jock's terrified yelps have become one long anguished wail of pain as the sea lion pins him and rips at him with his teeth. I'm sobbing as I run to him, my lungs bursting.

And then, out of the corner of my eye, I glimpse a streak of dark seal-coloured fur. I hear this crazed battle shriek, high-pitched as a banshee, and in a flash Moxy comes into view. She speeds across the rocks, whisks straight by me, and without an instant of hesitation she flings herself on to the back of the attacking sea lion.

The sea beast gives an almighty roar as my cat attaches herself to his back, with all four paws digging in claws. She looks like she's riding a bucking bronco, the way she's perched on that sea lion's back. I don't know if she's hurting him, but she's sure infuriating him! He lets go of Jock immediately and begins trying to shake her loose. He lumbers and twists to rid himself of Moxy, but she's attached like a vampire cat, fangs driven deep.

The sea lion turns as he raises himself up on his hindquarters and then, with a monstrous bellow, he retreats! He bounds back across the rocks, heading for the end of the reef, and I keep expecting Moxy to leap off and let go but she stays with him! She clings on tight all the way to the end of the reef until she's certain the sea lion is going to leap, and then, just at the moment when the massive beast launches himself full tilt into the ocean, she flies through the air. I watch the sea lion's massive wake rise up as he hits the water, covering her. Moxy gives a brisk shake to get the water off her back, her ears flat, and then with a yowl of victory she trots back across the reef to the point on the rocks where Jock is lying, panting and sore.

By the time I get to them, Moxy has roused Jock and has him back on his feet again, and we pick our way back across the rocks to Gus. Moxy touches noses with Jock, gives the wound a perfunctory sniff, and then, without any further ado, leaps up and takes her place on Gus's rump once more and begins to groom herself, as if she has never been away. Jock, limping a little, blood soaking the fur of his ruff and his left shoulder, takes up his position at Gus's heels. The four of us, wounded but reunited.

I look at the rocks where the sea lion leapt back into the water, and that's when I see the black speck on the horizon. My heart leaps because the speck is moving and it has to be a ship. It's the HMS *Canterbury* heading for South Bay.

CHAPTER 13

The Gates to Tartarus

How did Moxy find us again? I have no idea. I look back at her on Gus's rump, curled up in a ball asleep, utterly exhausted. Her tiny paws are ragged and bleeding from the great distances she's travelled since we saw her last. If only she could tell me her stories!

Without words, I have to hunt out the secret language of her adventures since we lost her in the river. There's a sliver of a graze across the top of her haunches, and a livid mark in her silver seal-pelt, and I know that must be the wound inflicted by Helen's arrow. It's as if the tip tried to pierce her, but Moxy, having been dipped in the river Siberia, was invulnerable.

There's a toothy bite mark on her left shoulder. A stoat, maybe? What else would be big enough or foolish enough to take her on? Even if she could, would Moxy tell me? She's always been a little mysterious. I guess I'll never know what she did in those days after we lost her.

She's worryingly thin. Moxy was never a fat cat, but now I can see all of her bones, can count the ribs protruding.

She's so deep in slumber that as we rock along over the goat track that takes us from one cove to the next, she's like a limp doll, dead to the world, and I worry she is actually going to fall off. As we round an outcrop right near the sea, I look back over my shoulder and see her slipping all the way to one side of Gus's rump. It's only good fortune that Gus straightens up just in time and changes direction on the track, and then as soon as he begins to lurch the other way Moxy slides again in that direction and nearly tumbles off the other side!

It's too much to watch and I know I'm being over-protective but what if she slips off and plummets into the sea below us? I can't lose her again.

I bring Gus to a halt and gently pick her up off his rump. Moxy rouses from her slumber and gives a yowl of displeasure at being lifted away from Gus. I unzip my sweatshirt and stuff her inside so that she's pressed up against my chest like one of those babies in a papoose being carried by their mother, and once she's inside the sweatshirt she starts purring. She likes being close, her fur against my skin. As she drifts back to sleep, she reaches up with her little face and gives me one of her love-bites, nipping me gently with her jaws, clamping delicately, affectionately on to my chin. I know she's saying in her own way that she's missed me and she's glad to be back.

Gus is tired. I can feel the languor of his strides. We have maybe an hour to go before we reach Kaikoura and right now the HMS *Canterbury* is moving steadily onwards to South Bay.

I'm trying to stay calm, to tell myself that the boat will take a while to reach its destination and drop anchor, and then the people have to be loaded on board, so I don't need to panic. Yes, it will be close if we stay at this pace, but if I push my companions too hard, we won't make it at all. Jock's favouring his left leg. I've washed the wound as best I can, using salt water straight out of the bay, but already it's swollen up and I'm worried that it might be getting infected. The gash keeps seeping so that the white fur on his shoulder is tinted bright red with blood.

Jock limps on at Gus's heels, and when we ride the goat track where the path becomes too narrow he drops back and trails behind us. We squeeze between bushes of cutty grass and then we come round the sea cliff so at last we can see the black sands of Peketa. The very last beach that we must cross before we arrive at our destination.

Gus makes grunty noises, sing-song like he's whistling a tune as we go downhill to reach the black sand. I lean right back, almost lying flat on Gus's rump so that he can balance himself. It's a steep trail down the clay cliffs – and then at last we've reached the beach. The tide is halfway out, the sand still wet and firm beneath us. Black and white stilts with red legs stalk up and down the beach in front of us as we walk by, looking surly, as if our presence is bothering them. Maybe it's nesting season and we're in their territory, or maybe they just like to be grumpy. They look like angry old men with their shoulders hunched and their eyes beady on us as they stomp back and forth and refuse to get out of our way.

The bay is a clean stretch of black sand ahead of us. To the inland side, the beach becomes boulders, impossible to ride on, leading up to the hills above. To the right-hand side, the sea is at half-tide, lapping against the sand. Ahead of us, I can see the gap between the trees at the end of the beach. We're almost there now. That next bay beyond is South Bay where the HMS *Canterbury*, no longer on the horizon, must already be dropping its anchor.

We're halfway down the beach when my early warning system goes into full alert. Jock gives a gruff bark that becomes a disturbing, guttural growl. I know the sound so well now – it's the one he makes when an aftershock is coming. This is different from the other times, though – the bark is deeper, the growl has more menace to it. He's like a werewolf, transmogrifying in the light of a full moon. The growl becomes a howl, violent and baleful, and then Moxy joins in too and she is yowling, and Gus stiffens underneath me and he raises his head up and his ears flatten. When I hear the boom this time it's so loud! It's like a sonic blast in the hills above, and then, racing after it, the freight train comes roaring through beneath us.

I remember that when the seven-point-eight quake struck, one of the most terrifying things about it was that I couldn't see anything. I was totally blind to the onslaught of the earth's power. I had no eyes to comprehend the world around me and everything was noise and motion in blackness as the house bucked like a rollercoaster beneath me, the deafening sound of the ground roaring below.

This time I can see the devastation as it happens. The ground is being ripped apart, the sweep of coast ahead of me cracking like an eggshell, giant fissures opening in the black sand. Chasms wide enough to swallow a horse, deep enough to take us all to Hades.

Willard Fox help me! I have no protections! The backpack is gone and there are no braids in Gus's mane. And now the earth is going to swallow us all!

I start to scream, but my cries are drowned out by the roar of the train. There's this biting pain, as if a vice is gripping my chest and it won't let go. I think maybe I'm having a heart attack until I realise it's Moxy, who's woken up to find the earth shaking apart and in her panic has extended the talons on all four of her paws and limpeted herself on to me.

As the pain grips my chest, I feel things change underneath me and Gus does too. He splays his four legs to keep balance, but the earthquake is shaking him in every direction. Suddenly, the earth itself gives a violent, rolling buck and Gus reacts with a crazed whinny and goes up on his hind legs! As he rears, I stay with him and grip desperately with my hands to the saddle pommel.

Gus rears so high up that for a moment I think we're going to be tipped over backwards and he'll come down on top of me. Then the earthquake slams him on to all fours again and as I come back down with him I feel my stomach smash into Gus's neck. I'm winded by the blow, gasping for air.

Beneath me, Gus gives a panicked snort, nostrils flared wide. He looks down the length of the beach ahead of him where the eggshell cracks are multiplying in the sand, and in that split second his equine instinct takes over. He bolts.

I'm still gasping for air, weak and shocked by the blow to my gut, and I'm like a sack on his back. I've got no balance, I'm barely capable of clinging on, and there's nothing I can do to stop him.

So I hang on for dear life and my ears fill with the train-roar. When I finally manage to raise myself in the saddle and look ahead of us I am struck with terror. The smooth stretch of black sand that blanketed the bay just moments ago is changing shape before my eyes. The earthquake is splitting the sand apart in great fissures. Along the entire beach, giant cracks are beginning to open up. It's as if the sand is shattering like glass, splitting wide, as cracks like chasms spread in a great sweep down from the boulders all the way to the sea!

"Gus!" I force myself up in the saddle and dig

down my heels, thrusting hard against my stirrup irons to give me the strength as I struggle to pull on the reins.

"Pull up!"

I can see the first sand chasm looming ahead. Gus is in full gallop and he's not listening to me. The instinct in him to run, the primal urge, is stronger than my power over him. I'm still gasping for air, winded and exhausted, and my tired arms cannot possibly hold him back. I'm screaming against the train-roar, yelling at him to stop, holding on for dear life. And even now I think it's too late to stop him. I can see the edge of the chasm and from the distance I try to look into it, down into the void that looms ahead. I wonder how deep it goes, how far we will fall before we hit the bottom.

There's a place in the Greek myths, Tartarus, that's even deeper than Hades. Is this the gateway?

Then something kicks in. I stop looking down at the gates of hell and I pull myself together. Because Gus is not the only one with honed instincts, and although mine aren't primal like his, they've been schooled into me. The athlete's mindset, my eventing brain hardwired into me by years of training ever since I began riding, suddenly takes over. As we approach the chasm, it's like a switch flips in my mind. I'm not on the beach any more, I'm at the One-Day Event and I feel this sense of calm as Gus goes into the start box. I can see myself setting my stopwatch, tightening my back protector, looking at the first fence across the field and listening to my mother's voice.

Evie, remember at the ditch – look up! Never, ever look down or he'll stop. Your eyes will take you where you want to go!

There's a chasm in front of me and for all I know it splits wide open all the way to Tartarus. What I do know for sure is that if I look into it, I'll end up inside it, because Gus will follow my eyes. Since we can't stop in time, since there is only one choice, I must look up. My eyes switch to the horizon and I wrap my legs tightly round my horse and instead of holding him back as I've been trying to do since the quake struck, now I urge him on, asking him to increase the power in his strides. I move my body up in the stirrups so I'm standing in two-point position and grab hold of a hunk of Gus's mane, just in case I get left behind by what is to come. Because I know now, we have no choice. We have to jump.

At the chasm, I nearly abandon my bold new plan and pull him up at the last second, because when I look ahead across the sands I realise what we are about to confront. This isn't just one sand chasm. The entire beach is splintering apart – even if we do clear this chasm, there are so many more to come! How can we possibly navigate the entire beach? But then I think about what Willard Fox taught me, how riding cross-country is a lot like beating OCD. You tackle the course one fence at a time. You don't think about the future, you stay focused on the hurdle that lies immediately in front of you.

So that's what I do. I assess the obstacle, judge my striding, and then I give a brief check on Gus to get him in the right spot to take off. Then I sit up and put my legs on and I ride it! I ride in so hard, it's as if I am a world-famous eventer approaching the first hurdle at the Badminton Horse

Trials. I hold Gus straight and I urge him on, and at that moment I feel the trust he has in me as his rider and suddenly we're working together on this, we aren't fighting any more. We both want the same thing, to go forward, to jump, to stay alive.

As we reach the edge of the chasm, I have to fight so hard against the urge to let my eyes drop and look down into the pit below. The urge gets worse when I feel Gus's hooves sink into the crumbling edge of the chasm and the sand starts to fall away beneath us. I think we're going down with it, but he takes off just in time and as the sand collapses we defy gravity and fly up! We are suspended in mid-air for that breathtaking moment, and then we're landing on the other side, solid sand beneath us once more. It isn't the smoothest landing. I'm thrown back and for a moment I think I'm going to fall. But my reflexes are honed and quick and I manage to grab hold of a chunk of his mane and keep my balance. When I look down I realise I'm clinging on at the point of his wither where the two braids used to be. As Gus surges forward I regain my seat and I put my legs back on and ride hard for the next chasm in two-point position, with my backside out of the saddle and my knees digging deep into the knee rolls of the saddle, heels low to keep my seat secure. There isn't much time to prepare – the next chasm is coming up on us fast.

This time we take it on a perfect stride, and I look between Gus's ears and can see the next crack opening up ahead of us. I put my legs on really hard because I know we're on the wrong leg and the striding is all wrong, and beneath me I feel my clever, clever horse do a flying change and adjust his stride, so when we jump it's perfect.

With each chasm that we're taking I can feel the power between me and Gus growing, and my fear falling further behind us.

I'm in charge, OCD, I'm taking the reins.

The next chasm is massive. On a cross-country course we'd call it a "rider frightener", because it looks terrifyingly wide – maybe two metres across.

Don't look into the void – trust your horse!

We clear it with room to spare and now we're galloping on and the roar of the train is gone, the quake is over and it's easier to hit our stride because the earth is no longer rocking beneath our feet, and no fresh hells are opening up before us. The only things we have to contend with are the obstacles that already exist, and now Gus and I have our blood up and we're riding this beach as if it's nothing more than a training course and we've settled into our pace and I never would have ever believed this if you'd told me, but we are having the best time! The wind is in my face and I can feel the power of Gus, and the sharpness of his instincts as he comes in boldly to each challenge and adjusts his striding and chips in an extra stride to make the take-off point, or stands back if he needs to and arcs over the ditches in a neat bascule.

As my pony's strides devour the sands, I feel exhilarated, as if this is what Gus and I were born to do. I don't fear what lies beneath us any more. I don't fear anything. I am alive in the moment, perfectly at one with my pony.

As we take the final chasm at the end of the beach, I let Gus pull up to a canter and then a trot so at last I can look back over my shoulder to check for Jock. My valiant dog is right there! He's been keeping pace all the way, making bold leaps over every chasm in our wake, and despite the injured shoulder he's on track right behind us, running for all he's worth.

"Come on, Jock! You can do it!" I call back to him as he comes in to leap the final sand chasm. My voice is lost on the wind but I know he hears me say his name because I see his ears prick up and his strides gain speed. He leaps and I see his paws scrabble as the sand caves when he lands, but then he's out the other side of the ditch and he runs to us. I pull Gus up to a halt now and all three of us are heaving, our breath coming in frantic pants, the heat off us bristling and humming like electricity.

I think, *Wow, my heart is really pounding hard in my chest from the adrenalin,* but then I feel this wild squirming beneath my sweatshirt and I laugh out loud because it's not my heart beating at all. It's Moxy. She wriggles and shoves her way up through the neck of my hoodie until her little face pops out the top and she gives a yowl straight in my face, a victorious battle cry. I know she's feeling exactly the same way that Gus and Jock and I feel right now, because we've been in a war and we have won. We've beaten the earthquake. We've taken ourselves to the limit and survived.

Panting and exhausted, we turn back and stare at the beach. The surface of the sand looks like it's been shattered by a giant's hammer. I can't believe that we've made it across without tumbling into those chasms.

We sit there for as long as we can, all four of us gasping in deep huffs of air, trying to get our breath back, trying to make sense of what we've just been through. And then at last I turn Gus, and Jock follows to take up his position at our heels, and as if it was nothing more than a cross-country gallop that we're putting behind us, we head on. Because there isn't time to think about where we've been when we still have somewhere important to go.

Up ahead of us, the very next cove is South Bay where right now the HMS *Canterbury* is about to drop anchor.

We've just ridden through the gates of Tartarus and we're still alive. We're alive and we are getting on that boat. All four of us. Together.

Only once the adrenalin has left my veins do I begin to feel the stabbing pains in my chest. I pull up my hoodie with the blood specks soaking through it and see the deep red gouges that Moxy made with her claws when she panicked as the quake struck.

Moxy bites my cheek, as if to apologise, and I smooch her right back. It wasn't her fault. We were all terrified in the moment and it feels right for me to have battle scars to show for it.

All of us have wounds. Moxy with her arrow graze, so thin and frail after her long solo journey, Jock with his bloodied shoulder where the sea lion bit him, and Gus, who has pulled up lame after his heroic gallop across the sand chasms. He pushed himself to the limit to get us through and I feel the soreness in him from the effort, his tired strides faltering as he distinctly favours his off hind.

We're all exhausted but we're so close now. This goat track leads us to the end of the headland. Any moment now, South Bay will come into view and we will see what we have been travelling towards for so many miles – the HMS *Canterbury* waiting for us.

"It's not much further," I whisper to Gus, leaning low over his shoulder. He gave every last ounce of his strength to beat the sand chasms, and he's totally spent. His body is wet with sweat, his neck where the reins have rubbed and chafed is crusted with the lather of white foam and his breathing is laboured and rasping.

And yet still he walks on. As we reach the end of the headlands I feel my heart soar as the blue sea of South Bay comes into view.

And there in front of us is… nothing. My eyes search the water in utter disbelief. There's no sign of the HMS *Canterbury*. No rescue ship and no people waiting on the shore. Nothing here at all, except the vast, isolated emptiness of the South Island coastline.

CHAPTER 14

Six Legs at Dusk

I choke down a gasp of despair as my eyes fill with tears. I saw the HMS *Canterbury* coming into shore! It couldn't have disappeared!

So where is it?

And then I realise. Our journey isn't going to end in South Bay. I had assumed all this time the ship would be dropping anchor here, where the big vessels often do. But watching from the shore it's impossible to pick the line a boat is travelling. That ship was never coming to South Bay. Its direction was always set further north, charting a course straight into the next bay, in Kaikoura township. That must be where it's anchored now.

The next bay! So now yet again there are miles to go. And the four of us are so very tired. So yes, I'm crying because I'm exhausted, but truly the tears aren't for me. I'm upset because I promised Jock and Moxy and Gus. I told them that this was our destination, and now I have to admit I mucked up and I must rally them once more, tell them that although they're weary, I need them to give me the very last scraps of the strength they have left. We have so much ground to cover, and no time. That ship has already anchored in Kaikoura Bay by now – we need to get there, and fast!

I look at my companions with their heads hung low, and I realise that if I'm going to ask the impossible of them, then it must be as their equal. Gus can't carry me any longer.

Aching and stiff, I slip my feet out of the stirrups and slide down from the saddle, running the leathers up.

"Hey, Gus," I whisper to him. "Change of plans. I'm walking with you now."

Gus has given me so much, tried so hard for me for so very long. Now, instead of riding him, I walk alongside him, our six legs standing together. No matter what happens, I will be there the rest of the way at his side.

As we move off there's a yowl from up above me and I see Moxy make a flying leap down from Gus's rump. She lands on the sand, right beside Jock on her soft paws, and then gives herself a shake and trots forward to take up her position at the head of our party. Then she turns back and gives a meow over her shoulder to all of us as if to say, *"Come on, then! Let's stop moping and get moving, shall we?"*

So now we are all walking in unison, across the sands of South Bay, making for the final headland that will take us to Kaikoura and the end of the journey.

***

The Pier Hotel is the first landmark that comes into view when you round the curve of the bay into Kaikoura township. It's a two-storey tavern, a local icon, plastered in dusty pink with picnic tables on the lawns. Usually the place is humming with people, night and day. They come here to order platters of rosy red crayfish, split down the middle, drizzled with butter and served with a salty, piping hot side order of chips. Today, though, the Pier Hotel stands desolate and empty. I call out as we pass to see if there's anyone inside, but nobody answers me. The front doors are locked tight.

There's a sea fog rolling in. And there, through the mist I see it. A grey monolith sitting lonely and vast in the deepest part of the harbour. The HMS *Canterbury*.

A wave of relief washes over me. *She is here.*

I stare at the ship. She's like a brick on the water, square, painted dark grey with radar turrets in the middle and enormous flat decks big enough for helicopters to land on at the front and rear. She seems impossible to me, like how do ships as big as this one even float when they're made of steel?

Has anyone seen me from the ship? If I yelled to them from here they would never hear me. My stomach knots at the idea that I could have made it all this way and they might still leave without me!

I can see the crew lowering inflatables off the decks and I notice that the sea is rougher and choppier than it was back in South Bay. The wind has changed and little white caps crest the waves. They splash up against the hull of the HMS *Canterbury*, and they fling the inflatables about as they hit the water below.

I'm so tired but I know we need to keep moving. As if to confirm this, Moxy starts yowling, insisting that we need to keep on if we're going to make it in time, and the rest of us obey her and fall in behind her lead, heading down the main road that will lead us into town. We can't go across the beach from here to reach the ship because the bay at Kaikoura is large, hard pebbles, impossible for Gus to walk on. Instead we stick to the main seaside street, walking past the beachfront houses and the monkey puzzle trees, into the town.

As we walk, I peer through the windows of houses. There's no one home. No one in the corner dairy either, and the pub is boarded up. No people on the streets and no sound except the sea wind and the chime of Gus's metal shoes on the sidewalk. We are like a posse riding into a ghost town.

On my journey from Parnassus I've seen the

damage an earthquake can do. I've seen fields turned upside down, cliffs falling away, mudslides and boulders covering the roads, giant pillars of salty rock risen up out of the sea. Now I'm confronting a different kind of devastation. It's like the Titans, the giants in the Greek myths, have held a running race through the streets and their enormous feet have crushed anything they touch. Some buildings have been razed to the ground, others look almost untouched by the quakes, and then you notice the cracks in their plaster, the broken windows, the buckled rooflines.

When Jock takes up growling, I know only too well what's coming. I feel my feet turn unsteady beneath me, and then there's the creak and groan of girders followed by a crash as a window shatters nearby.

We all stand still, waiting for the shaking to stop. Then we keep walking, circling round the newly broken glass so that Moxy and Jock won't get their paws cut. The weird thing is, it's not even a big deal now. Gus doesn't even startle this time. The Arabian blood that would normally put him on his toes has been beaten into submission by his absolute exhaustion. We're so very tired that nothing gets much of a jolt out of any of us any more. We're just putting one foot in front of the other and making our way towards the end of the town and down through the car park to the beach where I can see the crowds have gathered right up on the shoreline and three grey inflatable rescue boats are coming ashore to ferry the evacuees to the ship.

At the sight of me and Gus and Jock and Moxy walking towards them, a murmur rises up. There are people talking and pointing at us and then, through the crowd, a face emerges and I feel my heart choke with joy.

"Evie!"

Moana waves frantically at me and comes running across the pebble beach. Her two dogs, Black and Decker, catch sight of us too and come right behind her.

"Mo!"

I'm so relieved to see her that I start to cry. Moana is crying too, and when she reaches me she throws her arms round me and gives me this massive, tight hug. The Labradors are bounding around as if this is the most exciting thing that's ever happened to them. They jump up on me with their big paws and then wag their way round the whole group and greet Jock with their tails erect and ears pricked, sniffing muzzle-to-muzzle greetings. They try to greet Moxy in the same way but she isn't having any of it! She gives Black a clean swipe across the muzzle and he yelps and steps back, and Decker does too. Moxy might be tired, but she's still in no mood to be sniffed by any dogs except her Jock!

"Evie!" Mrs Mahuta is striding up the beach with a very concerned expression on her face. "What on earth are you doing here? You're supposed to be in Christchurch with your mum!"

I am stunned. Moana looks pleased with herself.

"I told you I would keep it secret," she says smugly. "Everybody thought you went on the helicopter."

"I never left," I tell Mrs Mahuta. "I didn't want to go without Gus."

And now she's looking at me with her eyes wide.

"You rode here?" She shakes her head in disbelief. "From Parnassus?"

She looks at Moana.

"Did you know about this, Missy?"

Moana looks terrified. "Yes, Mum."

Mrs Mahuta glowers at her. "As soon as we have somewhere to ground you, you're going to be grounded!"

According to Moana, her journey was just as bad as mine.

"It was really hideous," she says. "The inland road is so long and we had to go all the way to Waiau and then wait there because they kept closing the roads to a single lane. We were in a convoy and it took ages for them to let us past Mount Lyford and all the time we were driving the only thing we had to listen to was one of Dad's really awful CDs. Ugh! Then him and Mum kept fighting about the music because she wanted to hear the news on the radio instead. I was in the back with Arama and the dogs and they took up too much space and so I got really squashed and uncomfortable the whole time, and one night we even had to sleep in the car like that!"

She turns to me. "What happened on your trip?"

I smile and stroke Gus on his neck where the

caked-on sweat has now dried off, creating sea swirls in his fur. "Nothing much," I say. "Just the usual."

"They're taking down the names on a list and then they take people on the inflatables to the ship," Moana says as we walk to join the crowds. "You're only allowed to take one bag. Mayor Garry is trying to boss people around about what they can pack and everyone is getting really sick of him."

I can hear Mayor Garry's voice before I see him. He's walking down the row of people queuing for the inflatables, still wearing his fluoro jacket, the one from the road patrol, and now he's carrying a clipboard too. He keeps lifting up bags as if he's checking how heavy they are, and I see him reach for Scary Mary's bag and she just about karate-chops his arm off! It's good to see that they're not being nice to each other any more and everything is at least a bit more normal.

I search through the crowd, hoping that the one person I want right now will be here.

"Where's Dave?" I ask Gemma.

"He's down where they load the boats," Gemma says.

I can see the vet now, or at least the back of his head. He's busy sorting out a stack of cages with a woman in a grey boilersuit. I call out to him and he looks up and sees me. He stops what he's doing and runs up the beach to greet us.

"Evie?" he says. "I thought you left with your mum?"

I don't bother to go through the explanation again. Someone else can tell him.

"Jock's hurt," I say. "I need you to look at the wound for me. I think he's gonna need stitches."

Dave bends down and moves Jock's fur to expose the wound.

"It's a bad one," he says. "I'll get my bag."

He runs back up the beach with his kit and sets about cleaning the wound, sluicing it out with saline fluid to get a clearer look at it because it is all crusted over now with sand and blood.

"What was it that did this to him?" he asks as he works. "Another dog?"

"A sea lion," I say.

Dave stops dabbing at Jock's shoulder.

"Seriously?"

I shrug.

"I'm not even going to ask," Dave says, moving on to Jock's flank.

"And did the sea lion do this too?"

"Nah," I say, "a wild bull did that one."

"So," Dave says as he takes out his medical kit and starts to fill a syringe with local anaesthetic, "you've had an uneventful journey…"

It takes Dave ages to stitch the shoulder up. He does thirteen stitches and it isn't easy because Jock is awake the whole time. Normally, Dave says, with an injury like this, it would be general surgery, but you can't do that on the beach and so he has to do it all while Jock is awake with a local in the wound. My good dog growls a little bit but he doesn't try to bite Dave or anything, even though I know it's upsetting him like crazy.

"You're lucky he's alive," Dave says as he sutures the shoulder. "A sea-lion attack? If it was a full-grown male then it had the strength to kill him."

"He would have done," I say, "except he didn't get the chance because Moxy attacked him and drove him off."

Moxy doesn't have a scratch on her from the sea lion. She's got that thin graze where the arrow nearly claimed her life, but Dave lets me treat that while he works on Jock because it doesn't need anything more than a dab of antiseptic.

"Do you want me to give her a dose of tranquiliser for the journey?" Dave asks me. "It can get pretty choppy on the life boats and she'll probably panic otherwise."

I look down at Moxy's wise Egyptian eyes.

"No way," I say. "She's brave."

I'm not drugging her now. Moxy would never forgive me. She's going to want to be wide awake to see everything when she gets on board.

"OK," Dave says. "You see the boats coming back towards us now? They're prioritising children and people with animals first for boarding, so you could probably get on one of them with Jock and Moxy if you want."

He smiles conspiratorially at me. "That way you can nab a good cabin before Mayor Garry starts trying to allocate them."

"What about Gus?"

"It's OK," Dave says. "I can sort him out if you want."

I don't understand what he's saying. "Sort him out?"

"At the vet yards. There are facilities just over the road where you can leave him. The paddocks are well fenced. Good grass. There's even a goat in there for company."

Dave sees the look on my face.

"Hey, Evie, it's OK. If you want to come with me and settle him in before you get on board, that's fine…"

I shake my head in disbelief, totally stunned. "I didn't come all this way with Gus to leave him here!"

Dave looks at me. "What did you think you were going to do, Evie?"

I jut my jaw. "I'm taking him aboard. There's no way…"

The roar of outboard motors drowns my voice. The inflatables are back and pulling up to the shore beside us. In the two boats are two blue uniformed officers, an older man wearing white with gold epaulets and a woman in a grey boilersuit like the one who was helping Dave earlier with the cages.

As the officers in the navy uniforms pull both boats up above the waterline, the man in the white uniform and the woman in the grey boilersuit walk towards us.

"Got a few more animals for transporting?" the woman says brightly. Up until that moment I had assumed she was part of the ship crew, but then I see the insignia on her suit: SPCA.

"Hey, Janna," Dave says. "I want you to meet Evie Van Zwanenberg."

"Janna Bateman." The woman shakes my hand. "Is this your pony? Isn't he lovely?"

"This is Gus," Dave says. And then, "Evie and I were just discussing her plans to bring him on board."

I love Dave at that moment because he doesn't say it in a mocking way. He says it dead serious and I know from the way he's standing there, with his hand on Gus's wither beside me, that he's with us. He's got my back.

"Very funny," the man in the white uniform says.

"We're not joking," Dave replies. "Evie rode Gus all the way from Parnassus to get him on your ship. She wants to take him with her."

"Evie…" Janna bends down to talk to me as if I was a little kid, even though I'm almost as tall as her so it is stupid that she's acting like this. "Be logical, honey, your pony's not going to fit into the lifeboats."

I glare at her. "I thought the SPCA were here to save animals?"

Janna takes a deep breath as if this whole earthquake has been sent to try her patience. "We can take your dog and your cat on board, sure. But a horse is just impossible, Evie. We can't do it."

"Don't you have a bigger boat?" Dave asks. "Something we can load Gus on to, to transport him over to the ship? I could sedate him for the journey…"

"I'm afraid not," Janna says. Except she says it so quick, like she doesn't even care about pretending she's tried to think about it and she sure doesn't look at all sorry.

"Right," she says to me, "let's get your cat prepped to board. Dave will help you with the dog…"

And she actually reaches down to pick up Moxy! She must think she is sedated, or maybe she thinks

Moxy will like her. Of course Moxy takes one look at Janna, hisses like a banshee, takes a swipe that draws blood and then ducks behind my legs!

I reach down and I pick her up and hold her tightly in my arms.

"Forget it," I say.

Janna frowns. "You don't want to take the dog and cat?"

I cast a look at Dave who gives me a look back, like we both know that this woman is just not getting it!

"They're not going and neither am I," I say. "If Gus can't come on board then I'm staying with them here in Kaikoura."

"You can't do that!" Janna says.

Dave laughs. "You really haven't met Evie before, have you?"

Janna looks really furious now. "This a civil emergency. We can force you to come on board if we need to."

She turns to the man in the white uniform. "What do you want to do, Captain?"

So despite being bossy she's not actually in charge!

The man in the white uniform has been with Gus all this time, stroking his muzzle.

"Handsome lad, isn't he?" the captain says. "What breed is he, then?"

"He's an Arab, sir," I say. It feels right to say "sir" because of his uniform and stuff.

"Arab? They're desert horses, aren't they?"

I nod. "Yes."

"Well, Desert Horse," the captain says to Gus. "I guess it's up to you. So how about it... Can you swim?"

CHAPTER 15

Pegasus, Son of the Sea God

From the other side of the bay, when I looked out from the Pier Hotel, the sea was calm and the waves were dancing playfully, trimmed with little white caps. Now that we're here on the beach right beside the water, it all feels different. The tide has turned. The waves have risen up, the white caps have become high, frothy peaks and they crash against the rocks in the bay and lash against the sides of the gigantic grey warship that sits waiting for us at the deepest point of the harbour.

"Can your horse swim?" The captain asks me this

time. "Because if he can reach my ship, then we can get him on board…"

As if asserting its power at that moment, the sea smashes a gigantic wave on the beach and the roar of the surf nearly drowns out the captain's words. Two crew members make a frantic lunge to grab the inflatables as they are almost ripped away by the retreating tide.

This is not a calm beach, not the sort of place you wade in for happy summer paddling. The bay of Kaikoura is wild water. The Southern Ocean, treacherous and deep.

So can he swim?

I stare at the crashing waves in front of us and then I turn to my horse. Poor Gus! He's been so brave and so strong to make it this far. He's given me everything to get us here, to our destination. How can I possibly ask more of him?

I lean in close to his neck and press my cheek up against his, jaw against jaw, my face tilted up so that I can whisper close in his ear.

"Pegasus," I murmur softly so that only he can hear me, "this is the final task, I swear to you. And if you don't want to do it, if you are too tired to swim to the ship, then that's OK, it really is. You're already my hero, you know that, don't you? And if you don't have the strength left inside you to go any further, then we'll all stay. You and me and Jock and Moxy together. We won't go without you. No matter what happens, I will never leave you, I promise."

As I speak, I watch Gus's ears swivel and turn, focusing back and forth, listening to my words. I have my arms round his neck, fingers tangled in the silver threads of his mane as I hold him close, and I know he understands me, because he does that thing where he gives me a shove with his muzzle as if to say, "I'm ready. Let's get on with it."

I hug him tightly one last time and then I let go and turn back to the captain.

"I need to take his gear off first. He can't swim with a saddle on him."

My life for the past week has been strapped on to Gus's back. Now I unravel the tiny universe bound on with rope and dressing-gown cord. I lift down the weather-beaten tent and the crushed-up sleeping bag that have been cinched on since Parnassus. I

208

undo the girth and slip the saddle off. Now Gus is unfettered and all that's left holding me to him, all that remains, is his bridle.

I look into Gus's eyes. Then I take a deep breath and I undo the throat lash and noseband, and then I slip the bridle off his head so he's bare. There's nothing to hold him any more.

"What are you doing?" Janna looks anxious. "You need to get a halter or something on to that horse now! How are you going to lead him into the sea without a bridle?"

"If I leave it on he'll get his legs tangled in the reins when he swims," I say. Anyway, I don't need to lead Gus. Him and me, we've discussed this. I've told him what's to come. He knows I'll stay if that's what he wants. Now Gus needs to make this decision for himself.

I walk to the inflatable where Dave is waiting for me with Moxy in his arms. He helps me to climb aboard and then he passes her to me.

"Jock!" My dog obeys immediately and makes a leap from the shore to the boat without getting his paws wet.

Dave gets on board with Janna and the captain, and then there's the stutter of an engine as one of the crew begins to start the outboard motor.

"No!" I call to the captain. "Stop it! We can't use the motor! It's too loud, it'll scare him."

The captain signals for the crew member to cut the engine. "We'll use the oars instead," he orders. "Row us out and keep it steady, give the horse time to follow."

The two crew members take up position in the middle of the inflatable, slip the oars into the water and start to row. The inflatable doesn't move much with the first couple of strokes, but then with a sudden thrust the boat begins to propel itself rapidly out into the sea.

Gus, who's been watching us all this time from the shore with his ears pricked, sees me and Moxy and Jock start moving away from him and gives a panic-stricken whinny.

"Gus!" I call back to him. "Come on, Gus! You're coming too!"

Gus whinnies again and breaks into a canter, storming down the shoreline and then turning and cantering back again, his eyes always on me. He doesn't know what to do. He raises his head and gives this shrill, high-pitched clarion call, as if he's demanding that I come back to him.

"Gus!" I call again. "Come on, Gus! Come on, Gus! Come on!"

Gus plunges forward abruptly. His front hooves strike the water, but before he can go any deeper a big wave pushes on to the shore and swamps him so that all four of his legs are suddenly submerged in sea foam, and he jerks back in fright and continues pacing back and forth. His ears are flat against his head.

"This is ridiculous. He's not going to come on his own." Janna in the inflatable beside me looks furious.

"Gus!" I call again, and this time Moxy echoes my cry with a chorus of meows, as if she's yowling for him to come to her! In the boat beside me Jock, with his front paws up on the side of the inflatable, starts too, barking like crazy, and now all three of us are calling to the shore in unison.

"Come on, Gus! You can do it! Swim!"

Gus crab-steps back and forth on the shoreline.

In a panic, he rears up and stands on his hind legs and whinnies once more.

He crashes back down on all fours, and then, with a defiant shake of his mane, he ploughs into the water!

He comes for us, cantering into the waves. I'm shouting my lungs out, urging him on, and Moxy and Jock are baying like mad for him as Gus's legs disappear and the waves splash off his chest. Suddenly he submerges into the deep water and his rump drops and his head goes right up high, so all we can see are his head and neck. He's snorting hard, nostrils flared, making laboured grunts as his legs pump like pistons beneath the murky blue seawater in his efforts to reach the inflatable.

"Go, Gus! Yes! Good boy!" There are cheers from the crowd on the shore, and on the boat beside me Moxy and Jock are going berserk!

"Slow your pace down!" The captain instructs the oarsmen. "He's in the water! Give him time to catch us up!"

The rowers kill their stroke and as soon as they do it's as if the inflatable is being swept violently sideways in the grip of the sea current. Out here beyond the rocks, out the back of the surf, the water changes colour from pale ice to dark indigo. It's much deeper here, and the waves are so powerful against the side of our boat even Jock on his four legs is having trouble standing up.

I grip on to the side of the inflatable to stabilise myself, keeping my eyes on Gus. He's gaining on us fast, powering through the churn and swell, the waves battering him as he fights to stay on course.

"Start rowing again!" The captain gives the order for his men to pick up their stroke. They dig in with the oars and we're moving forward again, so that soon the shoreline seems a long way away. Up ahead the grey slab of the HMS *Canterbury* rears up out of the sea. It looks so big up close! The vertical walls of the ship are as tall as a skyscraper.

Gus is swimming now for all he's worth. His eyes are on me and I keep calling to him the whole time, even though I'm losing my voice and sometimes fear almost chokes me as I watch him struggling to keep his head above the waves. When he strikes a big swell that sweeps right over his head there's a moment when he disappears completely beneath the water.

"Gus!" I hold my breath for what seems like forever, and then there he is! His ears are soaked and his eyes blink in the salt water, but he's still with us!

"Good boy, Gus! It's not much further!" I call to him.

I look back over my shoulder at the square hulk of grey gunmetal looming up in the sea ahead of us. The waves are slapping violently against the hull of the ship, and as we come alongside the captain is issuing orders to the crew on board, and ropes are being lowered to us to secure the inflatable. "Harder to starboard!" the captain is calling.

We've made it to the ship, but now I can see the exhaustion consuming Gus. He can't last very long out here, treading to stay afloat in the freezing cold water. His endurance has finally reached its limit.

We need to get him out. Fast.

The captain has a walkie-talkie and he's talking to the crew members above us on the deck. I watch as they swing round the pulley they use to lift the inflatables in and out of the water and lower the canvas belly band that will be used to winch Gus on board.

The captain takes hold of the canvas and turns to Dave. "We need to get this round his waist."

Dave looks at Gus in the water beside the inflatable. My pony has sunk deeper and he's struggling now to keep his head above water.

"Evie, can you keep him steady while we drop the band into the water, and then we can hook it up from the other side?"

"OK," I say.

But when I get Gus close to the boat, the waves keep pushing him into the inflatable and then dragging him away. Sometimes when a big wave hits, it pushes Gus dangerously between the inflatable and the hard metal of the hull of the HMS *Canterbury*. We're waiting for the crew above to give the all-clear that the pulley is ready so we can hook it round the belly band.

"Get them to hurry up," Dave says to the captain. He looks at me and I see he's afraid too. He knows that Gus can't do this much longer.

The crew signal that they're ready and Dave grabs

the shank of the belly band, and the chain of the winch lowers and the band drops into the sea. I watch as the crew struggle to work with grappling hooks from the other side to catch on to the band beneath the water and pull it up the other side of Gus, but it's impossible.

"How can we get it underneath him?" the captain is shouting at the crew.

"I don't know," the First Mate shouts back. "We've never had to bring a horse on board before!"

Gus is pressed up hard against the inflatable and I see the fear in him, the whites of his eyes flashing as he flails about, fighting against the waves that threaten to slam him into the bow. In my heart I know the truth. He will die out here in the deep water. He'll never make it back to shore – it's too far away for him now. He will die unless we get him on board that ship.

I stand up and go to the side of the inflatable.

"Dave!"

He's been struggling with the belly band but he stops.

"Evie." He looks devastated. "I'm sorry…"

I thrust Moxy into his arms.

"Look after her for me?"

"Evie? What… what do you think you're doing?"

I strip off my boots, jods and hoodie so that I'm in just my T-shirt and knickers. Then I grab the end of the belly band and take the loop of it and secure it round my ankle.

"I'm diving underneath him." I step up on to the side of the inflatable. I wobble perilously as the sea almost rocks me straight off the side!

"Evie!" Janna says. "Get back in the boat now and let them handle it!"

I feel Dave's hand on my arm, but he's not pulling me back into the inflatable, he's holding me steady at the edge. He looks worried, "Evie?"

"It's OK," I say, choking back my own fear. "I can do this. I swim pretty well."

And then, before anyone else can try to change my mind, I leap.

The shock of the freezing water knocks the wind out of my lungs as I strike the waves. I've jumped in feet first and as I bob up again I'm struck in the face by a wave, and I feel Gus's body slam up against mine. I am wedged in between him and the inflatable. I try to make enough space between us to dive without being struck by his hooves, but the sea is pushing against me and all I can do is cling with one arm to the boat and wait until a wave creates a gap between us. Gus is struggling in the water beside me, exhaustion overwhelming him so that he barely acknowledges that I'm beside him.

"Gus," I say. "Hang on…"

A big wave sweeps over me and I hear the captain shouting "Evie!" and I know I have to go now or they'll drag me back into the inflatable. I take a deep lungful of air, push off from the boat and kick away from them and I dive…

***

When Miss Lowry made us do our project about the Greek gods, I did mine on Pegasus. Even though Pegasus worked for Zeus carrying the thunderbolts, his father was actually Poseidon the sea god. Because Poseidon doesn't just control the ocean – he is also the god of horses and the god of earthquakes.

I know there aren't really any Ancient Greek gods watching over me. Just the same as I know that just because I'm OCD I don't truly possess the power to bring the earth to its knees and destroy the world. I swear, though, that as I dive down beneath Gus with the belly band strapped to me, the sea that has been churning all around me until this moment suddenly turns dead calm. It's so still under there that it's eerie and I look upwards, blinking. Everything is so clear and blue that I can see through the ocean, as if the whole undersea world has been illuminated for me. I can see Gus's hooves sweeping through the water right above me and I duck my head so that I won't get struck. I keep going, deeper and deeper, until I can safely change my course, then I swim beneath him, until I'm on the other side and I'm climbing back up towards the surface again. I'm kick-kick-kicking as my lungs start to fail, and I feel the tug of that belly band at my ankle as the canvas strap is dragged behind me in the water. I'm close to the surface now, the blue water above my head is becoming clear, turning to sky as I break through and emerge gasping, desperate for air. I reach down and pull the band from my ankle and pass the hook across to Dave, who anchors it back on itself and tightens off the strap.

"We've got him!" He calls up to the crew on the deck above. And then to me he says. "Go wide when you swim back to us! He's going to start thrashing when the band tightens!"

I tread water beside Gus for a moment to make sure the strap is secure as they tighten it, and the winch takes the strain. Then I kick off against the side of the ship and begin to swim round Gus to get back to the inflatable.

As I stroke against the waves I can see Jock leaning over the side looking anxious. Janna is being useful for once and has hold of his collar because she can see that my dog wants to jump in and help me. Moxy is meowing like mad and squirming in Dave's arms, trying to get to me. The captain grabs me and drags me back on board and I collapse on the wet rubbery floor of the inflatable, gasping for air.

I'm lying there on my back, looking up at the sky, when I hear them start the engine on the winch. The crew up above on deck shout commands as the chain starts to retract and the winch gears grind, and then, in the clear blue above me, from out of the sea comes Gus, rising up into the sky.

He's airborne, and yet it's like he's still swimming, his legs churning. Dangling in mid-air, it looks as if he is cantering towards the clouds.

They raise him until he's right above my head. Then they swing the winch and Gus is still cantering as he's flung high in mid-air, swooping above the top deck of the ship and across the bow. He looks at that moment as if he's actually flying.

As the sunshine strikes him, his dapples glisten and his silver mane and tail flow behind him. He is truly magical. He is the Greek myth come to life. The winged horse, thunderbolt carrier, son of Poseidon. My very own Pegasus.

CHAPTER 16

Coming Home

I walk the blue line that leads to Willard Fox and feel a rush of nostalgia at the familiar stomach-churning aroma of hospital wards. The cleaning fluid and antiseptic that combine into that unique, unforgettable sense memory.

It's been a month since I walked these wards and nothing has changed.

Actually, that's not true.

Something has changed.

Me. I've changed.

I walk the blue line today and I'm not counting my footsteps. In the tiled foyer I don't fret about whether I will step on the cracks. When I get into the lift I press the button *once* and I smile to myself: *I'm in charge, OCD. I'm taking the reins.*

They say an event like an earthquake can trigger an anxiety disorder. Post-Traumatic Stress they call it. When the seven-point-eight struck, coming on top of my OCD like it did, was it really so crazy to believe I was the one who had made it all happen? That if I didn't stick to my rituals, I had the destructive power to make the earth shake off its axis? The bringer of earthquakes. That was me then. It isn't me any more.

"Evie!" Willard Fox sticks his head out of the office and calls down the hallway to reception. "My famous patient! Come in here before the paparazzi turn up, for God's sake!"

I blush with embarrassment as he says this, and the nurse at reception looks up. "How is that darling grey pony of yours doing?"

"He's good, thanks!" I return her smile with a shy acknowledgement as I dash past. I still get embarrassed when people recognise me, but it's nice when they ask questions about Gus. I'm not really the famous one – he is.

223

I never realised it at the time, when they were pulling Gus up from the sea and on board the HMS *Canterbury*, but one of the ship's crew was filming the whole thing on his phone, including the bit when I dived underwater to put the belly band on him. When the video got uploaded to social media, it went viral and almost overnight there'd been, like, a million people all over the world watching Gus on YouTube. By the time we docked in Lyttelton, there were TV news crews waiting to interview us, and they wanted to film Gus being unloaded from the ship. I think they were disappointed that he didn't have to fly a second time – the port at Lyttelton has a really long wharf and the ship just pulled up alongside so I could walk Gus off straight down the ramp.

My poor Gus! He hadn't eaten for two days by then, because there was no food for him on board. They weren't expecting to rescue a horse so it wasn't like they had any grass or hay put aside on the ship, and I didn't want to feed him human food in case he got colic. Even though I explained this, I still caught one of the crew trying to feed him a sausage roll on the second day at sea, and I had to explain to him how horses were vegetarians, but while I was explaining this Gus actually took a big bite out of the sausage roll, which kind of undermined my argument! I think he mostly got the pastry.

The crew radioed ahead to Christchurch to let Mum know I was safe. She was still in hospital then, but she was feeling better and they let me speak to her. I thought she'd be angry with me, but she sounded proud on the phone as I told her the stories about our journey. I left out the most dangerous bits as I didn't want her to worry. "You sound like my old Evie," she said. "Just try to stay out of trouble for the next forty-eight hours until I see you, OK?"

I didn't get up to much on the ship. Mostly I just kept Gus company on the deck. The crew had built him his own stall, using the squabs off the life rafts, strapping them together like a big padded cell to corral him in. They built the enclosure right up near the front of the top deck so Gus was able to look out to sea. I would sit on the squabs with him and watch the sea foam splashing off the prow, and it felt like we were Greek heroes, returning home from our odyssey at last.

Jock, always loyal, stayed with us all the time we were on deck. Moxy would sometimes join us, sitting up there in her old position in the indentation of Gus's rump. She'd make herself comfy and stare out at the horizon with that noble Egyptian face of hers, all haughty and important, as if she were the captain of this mighty vessel, surveying her course for home.

Mostly, though, she roamed the ship on her own. She pretty much had the run of the kitchen and got fed the best titbits by the chef, and all the crew adored her, especially the captain, who made sure she got set her own place in the mess hall at mealtimes. In between meals, she would cruise all the cabins as if she owned the place and hang out with everyone. I would hardly see her for hours at a time, but at night I'd hear her yowling at my door to be let in. She would trot through the door when I opened it and leap up on my bunk and sit there purring, waiting for me to join her, then when I got into bed she'd curl up on my chest like it was old times and give me love bites on the chin.

Having Dave on the voyage to Lyttelton proved to be crucial when Jock's shoulder got infected. Apparently it's common for animals to die from the infection after a sea-lion bite, which I didn't know, but Dave gave Jock antibiotics as soon as it looked bad and he was fine. He's a pretty good vet, Dave, at least I think so. A pretty good doctor too according to Mum. He was totally right about her broken pelvis. The doctors at Christchurch Hospital had to operate when she got there and they put titanium bolts into her. She's still got them in there now, so she says if we ever go through customs she'll set off the metal detectors.

The subject of the metal detectors came up because Mum thought that maybe, after everything we'd been through, we should go on a holiday somewhere, like the Gold Coast, just her and me. After all, it wasn't like we had a home to go back to. Our house was destroyed and we still didn't have a plan.

I didn't want to go anywhere, though. I didn't think I could handle being separated from Gus and Jock and Moxy for a single minute. So Mum agreed and we've stayed here in Christchurch while the insurance assessors figure out how they're going to rebuild our house. We've got a room at the Riccarton Racecourse Hotel, and from my window I can see straight out over the track and watch the horses early in the morning when the mist is still low on the ground, riding their gallop workouts.

The stables are right next door and Gus lives there with the racehorses. The hotel lets us keep Moxy and Jock with him too, and sometimes when no one is looking I smuggle them both up to my bedroom and we lie in bed together and watch movies and eat snacks. Moxy loves potato crisps.

I go down to the stables most mornings, way before breakfast, just as the jockeys are finishing track work, to hang out with them and smell that sweet, heady aroma of the horses, all hot and sweaty from their workouts, being cooled down before they hit the wash bays. I think the jockeys know I'm homesick for my farm, so they're all really nice to me. They treat me like I'm one of them and tease me and say I should become a jockey. I guess I'm small enough and light enough. But eventing is still my dream.

I remember the first time I met Willard Fox, I admitted to him it was my goal to become a pro eventer. So that's one thing about me that hasn't changed!

I take up my old position on the sofa opposite Willard and he smiles at me. "So, Evie," he says, "long time no see. Been up to anything lately?"

I laugh. And then I start at the beginning and I tell him all of it. As I'm telling him all the stories, of wild bulls and Moxy being lost in the river, and sea lions and sand chasms, I hear myself talking and I think, if I didn't know it was true I would swear all of it was too crazy to have really happened. But if none of it happened then how did I make it all the way from Parnassus to Kaikoura and bring Gus and Moxy and Jock back home?

It's like when the Greek heroes came home after their epic voyages and told stories of the foes they had faced – the minotaurs and the cyclopses, the sea monsters and the sphinxes – and those stories became myths. So how did anyone know then what was fiction and what was real?

"One night, when it was raining really hard and I was deep in the woods and it was getting dark, I found this house," I tell Willard. And I'm telling him the story of Helen of the Hundalees, feeling like I'm back there in that hallway piled high with fusty old stacks of newspapers, and I see Helen on her hands and knees, muttering incantations as she restacks the piles that have been strewn about by the aftershocks. I really want to take Willard Fox to meet her one day, because he's helped me, so maybe he can help Helen too, and maybe it's not too late and she'll be able to leave the house and be a part of the world again?

"I left my backpack there," I tell Willard. When he looks surprised and asks me why I left it behind I shrug and I say, "I didn't need it any more."

Anyway, it's a really good session and I talk and talk and when the hour is up, Willard walks me to the door. Usually at this point he says to me, "I'll see you next Tuesday."

But this time he doesn't say that. Instead he puts out his hand for me to shake. "Goodbye, Evie Violet Van Zwanenberg," he says, "it sure was a pleasure getting to know you."

I don't understand at first, but then I realise – I'm not coming back next week. I'm not coming back any more.

Willard Fox, I could never have made this journey without you. I will always be grateful that you gave me the power to become myself again.

That's what I want to say. I want to say *Thank you, Willard, thank you like a million times over, for what you've done for me.* But I just can't get the words out because I'm crying too hard. It seems so crazy that when I started coming here I hated it so much and now I can't bear the thought of never seeing him again.

"You're going to be just fine, Evie," Willard Fox says. "You don't need me any more. But if that ever changes, then you know I'm in your corner, and I'll be right here."

And I know he will be. Waiting for me, at the end of the blue line.

Epilogue –

Six Months Later

Down here in the belly of the ship, you'd hardly know you were at sea. The roar of the engines drowns out the noise of the waves that smash against the steel hull, and the stench of motor oil and exhaust fumes hangs in the stale air.

This is an inter-island transporter, a passenger vehicle ferry, and the crossing we're making today is a three-hour journey through the notoriously choppy and dangerous waters of the Cook Strait, the narrow neck of sea that separates the South Island from the North.

I never thought we'd be on a ship again. When Gus and Jock and Moxy and I disembarked from the HMS *Canterbury* in Lyttelton, I considered our seafaring days over and done with.

My only goal since we moved back home to Parnassus has been to pick up Gus's training where I left off, hoping that it wasn't too late to qualify him for the eventing team for Champs.

The journey to Kaikoura had been the best possible fitness test, so I knew Gus had the stamina to make it round the cross-country course. Plus we'd done all that track work with the jockeys in Riccarton. Now my training focused on jumping and dressage. We'd lost a lot of time from our schedule, but I knew if we really focused and worked at it, we'd be ready.

The fences at Area Trials were the biggest I'd ever jumped, and when we came home clear after the cross-country, I had this grin from ear to ear. We went double-clear that day – didn't even graze a single rail in the showjumping, and we made the team. I know Mum was proud of me, but I saw the look on her face when I was lining up with Gus to get our rosette at the prize-giving, and I knew she was thinking about what lay ahead. Making the

Area Trials team for Canterbury meant that I'd qualified to go to National Champs. And the announcement had been made that the Champs this year would be held at Taupo NEC – in the North Island.

There's only one way to get from the South Island to the North with a horse, and that is on the car ferry that leaves from Picton. The only problem was, State Highway One between Kaikoura and Picton was still shut, so instead of the normal three-hour drive from Parnassus to get to the Interislander, the trip to get us here so far has taken us two days.

Yesterday we drove with a horse float across the Lewis Pass, a journey that took us up to the high summit of the mountains of the Southern Alps, where the roads were treacherous with sheer cliffs dropping away right beside the edge of the tarmac.

Sometimes, when it got really steep, Mum had the car in first gear just to keep us climbing, and when I looked out of the passenger window the whole world seemed to drop away into the depths of the forest-clad ravines below.

"I know you're an old hand at these dangerous journeys," Mum muttered as she kept her eyes glued to the road, negotiating the tight hairpin bends, "but I'm not quite the hardened hero that you are, Evie."

"I'm pretty sure heroes are allowed to be scared," I replied. And man, those roads were scary! I think the only one in the car who wasn't terrified by the Lewis Pass was Moxy. She loved it. She spent the entire journey with her paws up on the window, looking out and purring with excitement. Jock, though, was even worse than me and Mum. He lay flat on the back seat looking doleful and pretending the world outside the windows didn't exist, and he was such a cowardy custard that he didn't sit up again until we were through the worst of it and cruising down the gentle slopes of Murchison. We overnighted at the Wairau Valley, then this morning we continued on through Blenheim until we reached the Interislander car ferry just in time for boarding.

The way the Interislander works, they get you to drive on board through the back of the ship and then when you leave again at the other end you drive off at the front. Which is pretty smart. They guided Mum in with the horse float as if she didn't even know how to drive one, which is crazy because no one parks a float better than my mum. She pulled in behind the car in front of us and switched off the engine. I opened the door and nearly gagged when I smelt the car fumes. I could hardly breathe down here.

"How are Gus and Jock and Moxy going to breathe if they have to stay down here?" I asked Mum.

"It'll clear," she said unconvincingly as she fussed about getting her handbag sorted and a coat in case it was windy on deck.

"Evie," she said, "grab a jacket."

"Umm," I hesitated, "Mum? I'm going to stay down here."

"You can't." Mum shook her head. "It's not allowed. Passengers have to go up on to the deck. Animals stay below. You're not allowed to stay with the vehicle during the voyage."

"Why not?"

"I don't know, Evie," Mum groaned. "It's just the rules, OK?"

"Can I at least come down and check on them?"

Mum shook her head. "They won't let you below deck until we disembark."

Mum slammed her car door. I was still sitting in the car and when I didn't open my door and get out too, she opened hers again and glared at me.

"Evie? What are you doing? We need to get up on deck. They're going to shut the doors soon."

"I'm not going."

Mum groaned. "Oh, Evie, not this again!"

"It's OK. You go up, Mum. I'm going to stay down here."

"But Evie, you'll miss the whole trip!" Mum said. "You won't see anything."

I smiled. "I've seen enough sea, Mum."

Mum laughed. "I guess all four of you have."

She looked at Moxy who was giving me play-bites on my jaw and purring in my arms. "I keep forgetting that you four are inseparable…"

She threw me the car keys. "There's a bottle of

water on the back seat, and some potato chips. See you in three hours. Don't get caught. I'll bring you back some lunch."

***

They sound a siren when the Interislander is about to depart from the port, the final signal to let everyone know that they have to get out of their cars and go above deck. I got out of the car when the siren sounded but I didn't go up. I called Jock and picked up Moxy, and all three of us climbed in through the jockey door of the horse float to be with Gus.

That's where I am now – sitting on the floor eating my potato crisps with Jock lying beside me and Moxy in her favourite position on Gus's rump. The engine roar underneath us is kind of soothing in a way. The sound that worries me is the weird creaking and clanking of the ship as we move through the water. Like, what if they forget to close the doors and all the water comes in? And the smell down here is still really strong – diesel, salt water and car fumes. I know if Gus had been alone here he would have hated it.

There's been a patrol moving through the ship, checking all the cars to make sure no one has stowed away. They just came past us and this man actually opened the door to the float! I was reading my book and I only just switched the torch off in time so he didn't see it. I crammed myself up hard behind the door and I could see the beam of his torch as he circled it inside the float. He was about to shine it on me, and he would have probably found me too if Gus, Moxy and Jock hadn't all started up at him at the same time. It was hilarious! Gus was like, nostrils flared and snorting like a dragon, and Jock gave this really low, throaty growl, and Moxy, she was just furious, standing up on Gus's rump and spitting and hissing like a cat from Hades.

I saw her eyes, yellow like a demon's in the patrol guard's torch beam, and then I saw him step back hastily and slam the door shut again. I heard him right outside, his voice wobbly as he spoke into his walkie-talkie, "Yeah, nah " he tried to sound cool – "she's sweet. Nothing here, it's all good."

I waited until I'd heard his footsteps move away before I laughed out loud. Now I'm sitting here in the dark. I don't really want to risk putting my torch on again in case the guard sees me. There's maybe two hours to go before we reach the port in Wellington on the other side. I'll stay in the darkness until then.

There was a time when I would have been desperate for this voyage to be over. And don't get me wrong – I'm excited about our goal. We're on our way to Champs! I am so amped about what lies ahead, because I know that Gus and me are going to ace it. We're ready for this.

But there's another part of me, a deeper part I suppose, that feels like you could waste your life just waiting for the future to happen. Sometimes we're so busy anticipating things, we miss out on the moment that we're living in right now. Looking back, that journey to Kaikoura was the making of me. And I know that, no matter what is to come, in some ways I'm still back there on State Highway One, and a part of me will always be there. Even when I'm all grown up, I know I will still be *her*. I will be Evie Violet Van Zwanenberg, with her dog at her heels, her cat at her back and her horse underneath her, with the sea of Kaikoura glittering in the distance, listening for the boom and the train-roar, waiting for the thunderbolt to strike.

Every girl dreams of becoming a princess.
But this real-life princess has a dream of her own.

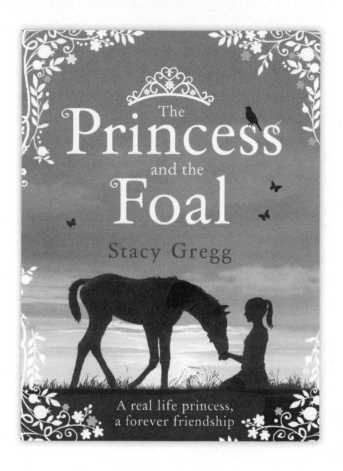

The
Princess
and the
Foal

Stacy Gregg

A real life princess,
a forever friendship

Discover the incredible story
of Princess Haya and her foal.

Two girls divided by time, united by their love
for some very special horses, in this epic
Caribbean adventure.

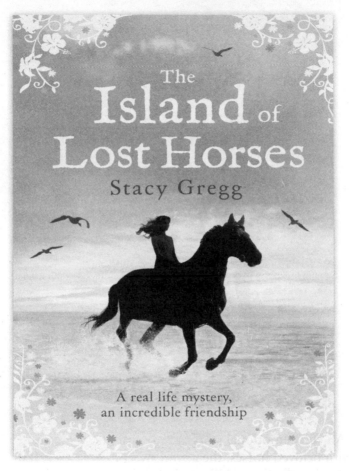

The
Island of
Lost Horses
Stacy Gregg

A real life mystery,
an incredible friendship

Based on the extraordinary true story of the Abaco Barb,
a real life mystery that has remained unsolved
for over five hundred years.

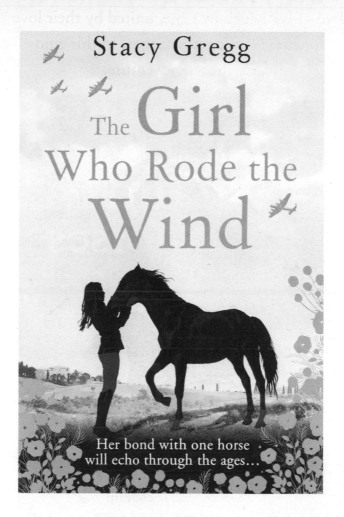

Stacy Gregg

The Girl
Who Rode the
Wind

Her bond with one horse
will echo through the ages…

An epic, emotional story of two girls and their bond
with beloved horses, the action sweeping between Italy
during the Second World War and the present day.

One family's history of adventure and heartbreak –
and how it is tied to the world's most dangerous
horse race, the Palio.

PONY CLUB
RIVALS

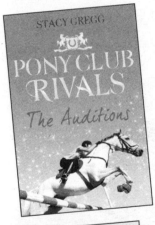

Don't miss

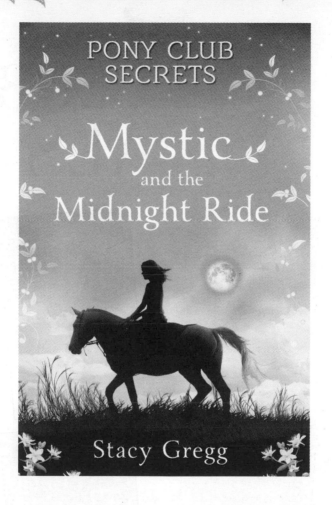

PONY CLUB
SECRETS

Mystic
and the
Midnight Ride

Stacy Gregg

Issie loves horses more than anything! And she especially
loves her pony Mystic at Chevalier Point Pony Club. So
when the unthinkable happens, Issie is devastated.
Then her instructor asks her to care for Blaze, an
abandoned pony, and Issie's riding skills are really put
to the test. Will she tame the spirited new horse, Blaze?
And can Mystic somehow return to help her…?

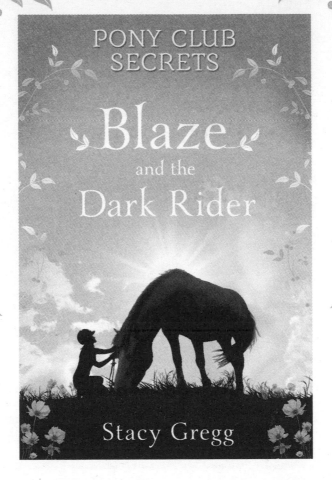

PONY CLUB SECRETS

Blaze
and the
Dark Rider

Stacy Gregg

Issie is riding for Chevalier Point Pony Club at the
Interclub Shield – the biggest competition of the year!

But disaster strikes when equipment is sabotaged and one
of the riders is injured. Issie needs Mystic's help again…

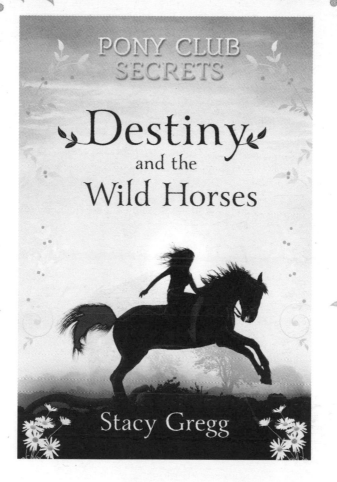

PONY CLUB
SECRETS

Destiny
and the
Wild Horses

Stacy Gregg

Issie and her horse, Blaze, are spending summer at her
aunt's farm instead of at pony club. When Issie hears of
plans to cull a group of wild ponies she's determined to
save them. This time, Issie is going to need
all the help she can get…

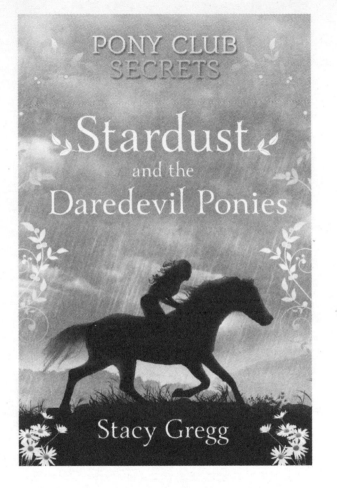

PONY CLUB
SECRETS

Stardust
and the
Daredevil Ponies

Stacy Gregg

Issie has landed her dream job – handling
horses on a real film set.

But what is spoilt star Angelique's big secret?
Could this be Issie's chance for stardom?